C. L. DONLEY

Amara's Calling

A Billionaire's Club Novel

First edition

This book was professionally typeset on Reedsy.
Find out more at reedsy.com

Contents

Join the Mailing List!

Get exclusive offers and content, learn about the latest news and releases straight from the author, and earn the latest freebies when you subscribe!
https://www.subscribepage.com/CLDMLLanding

1

Chapter 1

The very moment she opened the big double doors as she walked into work that morning, Amara Riley felt the electric current of energy. It followed her all the way upstairs to the third-floor wasteland where she worked, straight to her very cubicle.

Grayson Davis, the founder, and CEO of Webster would be in the building today.

Amara tried to consider herself immune to useless pandering, but she was helpless in its intense wake. Davis was one of her biggest inspirations and she considered him a kindred spirit from afar. She hoped to one day meet him and blow his mind with her innumerable achievements, intelligence, and rapier wit, but first things first: she had to actually figure out what exactly she wanted to do with her life to make that happen.

She wasn't so deluded to think they would ever meet or even lock eyes today, despite the fact they would be in the same building. He was the kind of untouchable you would expect from a young billionaire mogul whose striking good looks would have made him a celebrity overnight, whether his social media site had become a global phenomenon or not.

Sure he was one of those modern, hands-on types of CEOs, but she was pretty sure assistant to the assistant of the one of 50 project managers was not going to get a handshake and a "good job" pep talk today. Which is what made all the chatter on her side of the office so infuriating.

"Amy! You don't have any mascara I could borrow, do you?" Amanda, her cubicle mate appeared above her partition.

"None," Amara replied.

Amara was black and Amanda was a green-eyed, very pale redhead. Besides that, Amara didn't really wear much makeup at work, and Amanda had never before asked to borrow any. But she sensed the true reason for the ask was coming.

"Gahd, I can't believe I'm going to be such a mess when Grayson gets here." Amanda murmured excitedly, anxiously preening.

"Pretty sure it's Mr. Davis for us, and I don't think he'll make it to the third floor today," Amara replied.

"Should we tell him that Amy has a huge crush on him and would swallow his gravy?" piped up one of the guys in her cubicle, privately referred to as "the Dong Compound" by Amara and Amanda.

"Do it," Amara answered flatly.

Tittering was heard on every side.

"He would probably let her," Amanda quietly mused with a certain veiled contempt.

"He definitely would," one of the Dong Compound giggled.

"I would!" chimed in another from the corner.

"There will be no gravy swallowing, alright, now get back to work." Amara corrected, a bit too loud.

"Literally no one is working right now," Amanda offered over the snickering, "let's go spy on him."

"Girl, how many times do I have to explain to you, I can't go doing the same things you do? I will get fired," Amara sighed, exasperated.

"Come on, you're the only other straight girl on this floor, my uterus is completely restless right now. It knows he's here!" she faux whispered.

"Sonya said she would gladly un-gay herself for him," Amara replied.

"Just so he could support her massive weed habit," one of the guys added.

"What are we going to do, flash him our boobs outside the conference room?"

"Amara's sure to win that one," the Compound replied.

2

"Guarantee you he's never seen a pair of black boobs in his life," one named Justin chuckled.

"Pretty sure the internet is available to all Justin, and you're a fine one to talk," Amara said.

"OoooOoh," the Compound laughingly groaned.

"Not interested," he sent back.

"That's racist," she quipped. A few of them laughed.

Fate had the foresight to sit her alongside a group of knuckleheads that kept her laughing through the day and shaved off an hour or two of the daily grind. That and the amazing in-house cafeteria were the only things keeping Amara hanging on at Webster.

"Don't you want to see what he's wearing?" pleaded Amanda.

"Good God, can you two please go cream yourselves somewhere else?" Justin moaned.

"Excuse me," Amanda started, "Do we complain about the obsessive manner in which we have to hear about Jenny from the mailroom? Or Cameron in HR?"

"Or Shelly in Accounts Receivable?" Amara added.

"Yes," came the unanimous reply of the Compound.

"Well, now you know how it feels," Amanda sniped. "C'mon Amy, pleeeeease."

She was doing that thing every white girl that gravitated toward Amara since childhood did. Goading her into doing things outside her character, dangling promises of friendship in front of her in exchange for a fall guy. Leaning on their female solidarity so she could throw her under the bus later if need be.

This time, however, Amanda was giving her an out.

Judging by the way her life went, she would likely get fired by whatever silly shenanigans Amanda would get her wrapped up in today.

They were supposed to be two professional, career-minded ladder climbers, not giggling coeds with hard nipples trying to nab a husband Jane Austen style, or at the very least, some seriously hardcore child support for the next 18 years.

But Amanda had caught her on a particularly "fucks-free" day.

She'd been full of optimism when she was hired 10 months ago, the same week of her 25th birthday, confident that if she could just breathe the same rarefied air as Grayson Davis, she would be infused with his genius molecular energy and the drive to chip in at whatever position was available— anything to help further the machine she so admired.

But within three months she'd learned her job inside and out, and a familiar rigor mortis began to set in.

She was stuck. Again.

Turning cranks in yet another factory from morning to evening. Another company she had little to no desire to move up in.

Whatevs, Amara thought. This was the longest she'd ever been able to stay at a full-time job and she knew that her time here— in conjunction with her advanced degrees— would probably earn her another similar gig in no time. No one could land an interview like Amy Riley.

Amara on the other hand? She had less of a chance.

She always got a face to face. After that, it was touch and go.

If whatever Lucy and Ethel plan they were about to hatch got her fired for the first time ever, no future employer would blame her. Grayson Davis was sexy, brilliant, and intimidating. A visionary known to break hearts, sometimes even in person. When would she ever be in the same building as him again?

"Let's go," Amara said with a resigned sigh.

Her co-worker Amanda squealed, scrunched herself up with her fists in front of her and did a silly hop.

The fact that Grayson Davis happened to be here while she was having this exact epiphany felt like fate. She suddenly imagined herself in the company bathroom doing sexual favors in exchange for a glowing recommendation.

I don't work here anymore so you can't fire me, she'd say.

So cheap, she thought as the fantasy gave her stomach a jolt.

She no longer had the heart to imagine one day meeting him with poise and dignity. She was an overeducated slacker and it was all a pipe dream. The thought of catching his gorgeous blue eyes outside the conference room for a nanosecond was simply worth infinitesimally more than keeping this job.

"It's been nice working with you, Amara," one of the Compound said. His name was Ahmad, the only one that used her given name. He'd liked her a little bit, she could tell. He wasn't her type, he could also tell.

"Minority powers on!" Amara said to him one last time, bumping fists.

"No one's getting fired, relax!" Amanda sneered with an eye-roll, completely self-assured.

* * *

"So we see that in the next five years the growth towards social and technological synergy is expected to double."

As the department manager bridged his hands together in a presentation about synergy and workplace culture, Grayson Davis gazed beyond the frameless glass of the conference room, to the green expansive view of the grounds outside, his attention divided.

It occurred to him that his presentation was probably about an hour old. He hated that people constantly felt the need to impress him. He knew he wasn't giving off that air. It was more of an air of, "I am incapable of being impressed." Yet people always tried. Which in turn caused him to come up with more and more ways of seeming impressed. The whole thing was exhausting.

It sometimes made him long for his former life, the one where he was a fat ugly geek alone in his room writing code and creating programs. Back then no one was trying to impress him— indeed, it was quite the opposite.

Yet he was fairly certain he was the same person then as he is now. Funny what looks and a multi-billion dollar company will do to others' perspective.

He tried not to be bitter and mostly succeeded. His ambition would not have led him here without that experience, he understood. His painful adolescence had been a valuable training ground that gave him sympathy for a broad range of misfits and outcasts like himself. Ironically it gave him the passion for connection— to create a viable social network that relied on common goals and interests rather than geographical location. And rationally, he also understood that the bullies that made his life a personal hell growing up were not the same people that were now lapping up his every word. But emotionally, he observed that there was a very deliberate before and after pattern to his life, with the money being the separating line.

"If we're going to survive past 2020 we need to think beyond community to its immutable characteristic, which is family."

Well, that wasn't entirely true. There were always a handful of people that believed in him, like Dale his childhood best friend, co-creator, and COO. The rest of them had found his programming obsession the foreshadowing to a very sad, lonely life. Even his parents who — God bless them— declined the opportunity he'd had to skip whole grades, in the name of him being "well rounded." He'd barely scraped by every year, having completely given up on scholastic pursuits and focused his energies on crafting choice insults for his schoolmates, and hacking security companies until the wee hours.

Now he was rich, hot, virile, and had the world in his hands. And to be honest, it was a bit boring. All that fire in the belly, years working at Magellan with Dale— thriving and sculpting their passion project until 3 am until it became what it is today— was it all just so he could plateau at 34?

He did like being a leader, at least. Dale was the one to show him that he might actually be better at finding people's strengths than he was at exploiting their weaknesses, and it made him a great CEO, which he enjoyed.

But his life was not even half over. Was there nothing else to be done?

"I'm curious to know how you found this correlation between career demographics and Webster use among employees outside of the office..."

There was one advantage to success, however. And they were walking by the conference room in pairs every... oh, 20 seconds or so.

He smiled to himself.

Ten years ago, if someone had told him this would be his biggest problem, he would've laughed.

So. Many. Women.

They all intrigued him. Or at least, they used to. Like all natural phenomena, he found that women had patterns and could be learned. Yet they all seemed to consider themselves very special. But then he liked that. It was cute and one of the few genuine things about them. Some were naive, some were cynical. They all wanted love, no matter how low they cheapened themselves. That they couldn't seem to achieve the one thing they collectively wanted seemed to be a cruel joke to him. There were a few that didn't want love. And they were like category five hurricanes. It took a few too many lessons, but he'd eventually learned the discipline necessary to stay away from those.

A smattering of applause dissipated the cloud of his thoughts and Dale, his right-hand man, began concluding the meeting. "Any final thoughts?"

As every department head at the small table started rattling off redundancies he caught a glimpse of a very conspicuous pair of women walking across the length of the conference room. One of them was sharply dressed to the professional nines in a charcoal business suit and 6-inch heels, her shock of red hair cut into a bob.

And the other was Amy Riley.

Whose real name was Amara, but used Amy on resumes to ensure callbacks.

He knew this because he'd called his company at random as he is sometimes wont to do, and had a pleasant conversation with one Amy Riley.

He was Travis from quality control at the time— new of course, and had no idea what he was doing and needed help.

She was professional and helpful and clever and knew a bit more beyond what her job required, which was a rare quality these days in a lot of 20- somethings. What she didn't know, she'd had quick and credible solutions for. Plus she sounded sexy. Not that he would pursue an employee sexually. That would be unprofessional.

But he was curious.

He couldn't find her name in the company's directory and wondered if perhaps Amy was actually Riley, Amara J.

It was. He'd had to stalk her on his own social media platform to find out.

Though he was surprised to find she was African American, he was more surprised to find that she'd only been with the company 6 months at the time they'd talked. She seemed to identify as Amy only at work. The notion had made him feel guilty and then feel stupid about feeling guilty.

His company didn't engage in racist practices.

Did it?

She seemed to be obsessed with him, however, which flattered him.

Any quote she could find, any and every SPEC Conference at which he'd been a guest speaker was on her page. She'd put a blurb about how she would one day give him the interview of his life and how the world wasn't ready.

Humans are hopelessly social. Give them a platform and they will unwisely unleash any and all their innermost secrets. She posted fairly frequently and he wondered if she'd somehow done it in the hope he would see it. He'd thought maybe she'd be better suited as a content creator.

As the two women walked by, they sort of pretended at first to have some urgent business to attend to on the second floor— which was impossible, but slowly that facade seemed to be dissolving into giggles. Amara was the first to crack and almost instantly turned to go back the other way, with her friend clinging to her fitted white shirt behind her. Probably regretting her desire to stand out today. Adorably, about a minute later they returned, fully composed.

It gave Grayson an amusing idea.

He told himself that the idea had merit. Plus, he genuinely appreciated Amara's enthusiasm and wanted to encourage her.

"Hey Dale, let me stop you for a minute," Grayson broke in. "Can you get those two employees' attention behind you?"

"Yeah, they're from upstairs, I think? We'll find out who their supervisor is."

"No, it's okay. I actually want to speak to one of them... Amy I think is her name."

He loved doing that. He never once faltered. He was sure they thought he genuinely knew everyone's name and what they all were doing. He felt the energy shift positively. They liked working for him.

One of the directors near the door rushed out of his seat and called out Amy's name. Both girls turned around and Amara pointed to herself in disbelief. Cluelessly, the director tried to correct Amara, assuring her that she was not, in fact, herself, repeating her name.

Dear Lord, was this really happening?

He watched as Amy confirmed that she was indeed Amy. The redhead chimed in, "My name's Amanda..."

Oh, for fuck's sake.

"Amara!"

Amara heard her own name through the muffled glass.

Coming out of Grayson Davis' mouth.

CHAPTER 1

Oh. My. God.

2

Chapter 2

Amara gave herself a million notes as she made her way back down the hall to the entrance of the frameless glass conference room.

This is it, this is it, don't panic, be yourself, you were born to brush shoulders with this man, you are awesome, amaze him with your wit, but don't look like a desperate groupie, he probably wants to talk about minorities at his company, thank you God for making me black today!

She walked through the door and tried to summon that eerie calm that sometimes came upon her when, on rare occasions, she found herself in places of prominence. She almost had it, but then she looked around the room and the faces filled her with anxiety. What exactly was she here for?

She heard a calm voice at the head of the table say, "Have a seat. Simon, give her your chair."

Holy...crap.

Should she jokingly take a giant deep breath? No, that's stupid. Just sit down.

She gave an anxious look at all the people at the table who were oh so very high above her pay grade as if to acknowledge that she well knew the disparity between them. Inwardly she felt none. But it put them at ease.

You're about to look a gorgeous billionaire in the face, so drink it in she told herself. She did. She took a breath and looked him square in the face. She smiled. He smiled.

He was, in a word, beautiful.

His features were notably chiseled, a millennial version James Dean, even down to the angst which she attributed to his computer-nerd core. He was in a dark blue jacket with an argyle pattern shirt that was youthful, but the man underneath exuded power and leadership. She watched his dark blue eyes dance and it was all the things.

The people around her shifted. Lordy, was she an idiot?

She just gave herself entirely away. *People who brush shoulders with greatness do not soak up moments with them like they will be their last, dumdum. Pick a persona!*

"You're new around here, is that a fair statement?" Grayson asked.

"It is," Amara replied, nodding her head and looking down at the table.

"Where were you before this?"

"Oh, here and there. Nothing substantial yet just, still trying to figure out what I want to do."

"Did you go to school?"

"Boy, did I!" Amara joked, and they all laughed and loosened up a bit. "My bachelors is in English Literature, my masters is in Writing and Pedagogy."

"Goodness gracious."

"I'm so hungry, please sponsor me," she confessed with faux desperation. They all laughed again. She wasn't so naive that she thought her show would earn her a 12 rung promotion, but she was enjoying herself.

"I'm actually a fan of the humanities," he offered. "When we're on the brink of technological annihilation it'll be you guys who save us from ourselves."

"I just wish I'd saved myself a fortune like you did and just taught myself."

Wow. She'd done her research indeed. He was flattered.

"Well. Colleges have a vested interest in making sure you don't value the simple genius of the library until after you graduate."

A knowing hum reverberated through the room that was part genuine, part kowtow. And then the blatant, *what the hell is she doing here?* atmosphere began. She didn't dare ask.

"Do you see yourself having a future here?"

"Honestly?" she asked.

"Of course."

"Honestly... I'm thrilled to be working for your company, but I'm a bit bored."

You could've cut the tension with a knife.

You ungrateful negro, the white angel on her shoulder protested.

"It's no offense to anyone here and certainly I don't mean to suggest that should reflect on anyone else...it's not you, it's me," she smiled.

Since everyone else's jaw was on the floor she thought it wise to continue, "I'm not completely insane I assure you, it's just that...I was contemplating quitting today actually, because I just realized I'm taking up someone else's space who would really want it, because I'm so afraid to move on."

"So...your strategy is to do the same thing at another place, and spend the rest of your career as an entry-level employee," he posited, as a conclusion rather than a question.

Amara's pulse skyrocketed. Was she really in straight talk heaven right now with Grayson Davis?

This is real. He seemed to be genuinely concerned about her future, and good God so was she. *Tell me your secret,* she wanted to say. Though she was starting to suspect there wasn't one. He was brilliant and driven. And she was, well, addicted to her boyfriend Netflix.

"You know what? Honestly, Grayson Davis, sitting across from me and concerned about my future," she jokingly began. The conference room, while amused, was a little impatient to know where this was going. "I guess I'm relying on the fates to help me figure this out. What did men do 100 years ago when they found work? They saw a 'help wanted' sign, walked in, the sign came down, next thing you know it was thirty years later. It can't be that hard to find a calling."

"Only now this is the 21st century, and you're a young African American woman who's spent several years and several tens of thousands of dollars pursuing the meaning of truth, and the meaning of meaning."

Good heavens.

Amara's heart was beating in her ears, and though she felt an excitement on the inside— that was, to her, more akin to being near death than it was to arousal— she was pretty sure she was going to find out how wet he was making her once she stood up.

On the outside, Amara smiled.

"Touche," she simply said.

A beat of silence.

The billionaire took a breath. "Well, honestly I did not expect this meeting to go where it just went, thank you for humoring me, everyone. Amara."

"I'm sorry," Amara said, covering her face.

She wasn't sorry.

"Do not apologize, young lady." Good God, he was talking to her like a pervy uncle, he thought.

"If I'm here to talk about race relations they're great," Amara added hastily, with two thumbs-up held closely to her chest. "Ohmigod I'm sorry," she said again, hiding her face with both hands this time. Everyone laughed again, secretly grateful for the feedback.

Grayson grinned. It may have started out about race relations, but there was no need for her to know that. She was smart enough to gather as much. Anticipating needs again, Grayson thought.

"We appreciate that," Grayson smiled a killer smile.

She was on a roll and it was all going as well as it would in a dream. It made her think something else magical might happen.

It did.

"I'd like to continue this conversation with you in a more appropriate venue, so don't quit today, okay Amara?"

"Okay," she laughed, excusing herself from the table without another word as Simon held the door conference door open for her, obviously nervous. She covered the sides of her face with her hands as she vanished out of the sight of the solid glass windows of the conference room. Everyone still at the table could vaguely hear her saying curses to herself, which made them all laugh.

She was more capable than she let on, he knew. He'd spoken to her on the phone and inadvertently stalked her online. She was aiming for greatness but hadn't the faintest clue how to get there. Hell, with very little training and a little more confidence she could replace at least one person at this very table with ease, he theorized. His eyes unconsciously drifted to Simon at his thoughts who sat back down in his own chair, the first to break the silence.

"She's adorable," Simon said. The room nodded in muffled amusement.

* * *

As Amara made the long trek back to her desk she made note of the time. It was 10:08.

10:08 am on a Monday her life had changed in a flash.

And only a thousand more years until the workday was over.

Could she wait a thousand years to call her best friends Kim and Mya? Likely not. She had to coordinate that thing now. She could take an early lunch.

When she got to her desk, her co-worker Amanda was wide-eyed and looked sort of like she'd been crying.

"Oh my God, Amy! What happened?!" she shrieked.

"One second..." Amara stalled.

She powered up her phone, which she wasn't supposed to do at work, but it was an emergency. She waited for her personal Webster app to open. The cubicle was eerily quiet. Amara looked up and found all eyes were on her.

"What?" she asked with a furrowed brow.

"What happened? Did you get fired?" Justin asked in a whisper.

"No!" Amara answered.

"Well, what did he want?" Amanda was impatient.

"He wanted to know if I saw a future with the company."

"What did you say??" Amanda prompted.

"I said no, actually." Amara laughed.

All the guys dropped their jaws and their eyes widened as they met each other's gaze. Amanda was absolutely infuriated.

"I knew I should've been the one in that room!" she fumed.

Amara should've been offended but she wasn't. She could care less that a grubby opportunist was upset about her moment.

"What did he say?" Ahmad wondered atop the cubicle.

"Would you all like a complete rundown?" Amara answered.

They were all enthusiastic as Amara began, complete with gestures and voices and sound effects of the explosions happening in her brain. Suddenly she heard the familiar chirp on her phone of Webster notifications, one of which was a direct message.

"Hold on," Amara said, her head back on the initial task of setting up a conference call with her besties.

Her mind became that of a drunk's as she tried to concentrate on telling the story, messaging her friends, and also slowly comprehending what was staring her in the face: a direct message from Grayson Davis.

"Holy shit!" Amara said loudly as if in the throes of a crisis. It was a crisis. The cubicle farm was on the edge of their seats.

"He just sent me a private message..."

"Who, GRAYSON DAVIS??" Justin guffawed.

"I thought his account was run by bots?" Ahmad said wide-eyed.

"So did I," said Amara.

"It is," her friend Amanda confirmed smugly.

Even Amara expected something arbitrary when she opened it, but the message literally made her heart stop:

"Someone's on their phone during company time."

Winking smiley face.

"OhmyGodohmyGodohmyGodohmyGodohmyGodohmyGodohmyGodOH MYGOD!" was all Amara could chant as the phone made its way around the cubicle.

"What...the fuck, Amy," Justin said.

"I think he's like...for real trying to get some from you, Amara," Ahmad said, sounding concerned.

"Please God please!!" Amara prayed aloud.

"Honestly Amy, you'd let some billionaire just take advantage of you like that?" her co-worker Amanda spat, sounding disgusted.

Amara desperately needed to get a bat signal to Mya and Kim. She was in no position to use Webster and accidentally send something to the boss of all her bosses. She sent an S.O.S. text in all caps and hoped they weren't busy at work in the next hour.

Her phone chimed again, and Amara realized with a mixture of excitement and dread that she wouldn't be available in the next hour.

"Lunch downstairs in 45? I know it's early." Another winking smiley face.

* * *

By the time Grayson headed down to the culinary award-winning cafeteria for early lunch, he'd convinced himself thoroughly that his intentions toward Amara were completely and entirely professional and charitable.

She had been a delightful and unexpected distraction in an otherwise predictable headquarters visit. He didn't know what his expectations had been, but whatever they were she'd exceeded them.

She was kind of kooky. Like her profile. The only picture she had of herself was the profile picture, which was a blurry shot of her doubled over in laughter. Any other photos of her she'd been tagged in.

She didn't fawn over him outwardly like most women did, yet he knew firsthand how fanatical she was about him. Nor did she pander to him professionally with a Miss America answer about her future with the company.

No one would be surprised if the billionaire wunderkind took an interest in a potential bright and rising star. She'd sat competently in a room full of brown-nosers— talented ones, mind you— and stole the attention they'd all been falling over themselves to earn. By saying she was about to quit. Imagine if she became the next great mind at Webster, what a PR story that would make.

No one would suspect that during their first meeting he'd been busy putting a body to a face to a voice to a name, because her boring white dress shirt and forgettable gray slacks were still singing its praises like a church choir.

Nor would they suspect that inviting her to lunch had been any sort of inner battle between his professional self and his personal self.

Personally, he was a man who loved women. And women loved him.

It was a relatively late discovery.

An early misdiagnosis of bipolar disorder in adolescence demanded meds that made him fat and brought his already struggling interest in sex down to zero. When he stopped taking his meds his junior year of high school, shortly before dropping out, his libido was back but an incurable loneliness set in.

By the time he'd got a job as the youngest employee at the NSA, he'd gained the life of an attractive young male overnight, having shed the weight and much of his acne. And though his female co-workers had noticed right away, he remained awkward and solitary. It took another few years for him to confront his ignorance of women head on. Only then did he find out that his fears were unfounded, because as it turned out he was quite good at sex, and had since been making up for what he considered unforgivably lost time.

He became an avid researcher of women. Certainly not as predictable as BASIC or binary code but there were patterns nonetheless. He found sex to be mentally relaxing. He could let his body take over and his brain got more rest than it did when he slept. It was perhaps the one thing that he was naturally good at that actually interested someone besides himself.

Amara wasn't predictable at all. She was a complete mystery to him, but he didn't quite know why. He had to consider the difference in race as a variable. That and her intelligence was enough to cause a good number of unknown permutations.

He already had a type: blonde and buxom. Sometimes a brunette would do if she was foreign. He was never one of those guys that got excited by the thought of uncharted territory, and maybe it was just boredom, but something about Amara turned him into Vasco de fucking Gama.

Her body had to be the incentive. She was stunning, he surmised. First from her profile and then after seeing her in person. Her dreadlocked hair remained pulled back at work but he'd seen in her profile that it was usually variously styled and on display, as though it were her pride and joy. He'd seen in one of her posts where someone at work had warned her early on that her hair was "distracting."

Her doe eyes and her dark brows made her stare unignorable, a bit like Brazilian women, who were great in bed but a touch too dramatic for his taste. Her smooth features were pronounced and perfectly symmetrical. He was a sucker for symmetry. That and her height was enough to make her model material. She either didn't know or didn't care, he couldn't quite tell which. It sort of seemed like both. She didn't wear makeup at work. Or any adornments for that matter.

Was she a lesbian? Hot.

He'd slept with lesbians before and it was always memorable. He suspected some of them had just said they were to stand out, to make him chase them. Well, it had worked, and for the experience, he was genuinely appreciative.

He thought back to the humorous way she'd held her own this morning as if she were there to hold a press conference. The way she'd looked him square in his eyes sent a cool shock through him that he hadn't felt in maybe ever, as if she knew everything he'd been thinking and exactly why she was there.

He simply wanted to feel more of Amara's energy.

What would it be like to kiss her? Insane, he hypothesized. Her lips weren't as full as some women of color he'd met, but they still trumped any woman he'd ever dated. A smile formed at the corner of his mouth.

But still, his professionalism was in no danger, he assured himself.

Exciting people excited him and made the company better. That's all. And sometimes those exciting people were women, and yeah, he had a thing about women but...it's fine.

This was going to be fine.

3

Chapter 3

Amara put one foot in front of the other as she went down to the cafeteria and calmly set her expectations as low as humanly possible. *This guy is going to have Beyonce level attention on him at all times, so he'll definitely not be alone, and even if you were planning to get five minutes with him, better pare it down to 30 seconds in case everyone else gets greedy.*

She thought back to that moment in the conference room where his attention seemed almost like that of God having a conversation with His creation. The dude had serious presence.

He was filthy rich after all. And gorgeous.

Which made it all that more strange that he would be so attentive to one lowly employee who admitted to dreams of quitting. It had to have been some sort of... show.

But he hadn't asked the usual minority fodder. She'd had to volunteer it. And if the conference room was for show, then what was this?

Maybe a PR stunt? Shaking hands with the third-floor minority mascot?

Now you're just paranoid, she thought.

Or was she? Did he somehow know she was obsessed with him? How did he know her name anyway?

Oh Lord. Oh my Lord.

Amara's stomach lurched, and her knees weakened.

What the hell was this?

When she walked into the cafeteria, she wanted desperately to spot him before he spotted her, so she wasn't looking around like a freak and drawing the office awkwardness ghost into her space.

As she might've suspected, several of the tables had been moved to form one large, rather distracting table in the middle of the eating area. There was Grayson, wearing large black-rimmed glasses, making geekiness look the sexiest it's ever looked. He was surrounded on either side by employees, the COO Dale Abernathy sitting right next to him, whom she never found particularly sexy but the company he kept was doing wonders for him.

No one even looked in her direction, and she certainly wasn't about to saunter over there like the most popular girl in school when she was just the assistant to the assistant of the project manager.

"Amara!" she suddenly heard on her way to the salad bar.

It was him.

She smiled and tried to study the look on the COO's face next to him, but she couldn't read him.

He seemed to be summoning her to sit at the table, which didn't make sense since she was there to eat first and foremost. She wasn't there to sit and fawn over him in the company of his underlings. This was feeling very high school, and she didn't like it.

Amara was in no mood to compete for his attention for the next 50 minutes. The day had been magical enough, why tempt fate and risk ending on a sour note?

She decided to ignore him as she piled up her salad plate. Inwardly she sighed. The possibility of actually holding a conversation with Grayson Davis today was slowly dwindling. She shook it off. He'd been rich awhile now. He's allowed to be out of touch a bit.

She found an empty booth, out of sight so that they could each eat in peace without the pressure of expectation. She checked her phone for messages. Still no sign of Mya or Kim.

After 20 minutes or so, she got a Webster notification.

"Did you just ditch me??"

Amara's heart skipped a beat. She bit her lip, as if to keep her smile from completely tearing the muscles in her face.

Was that going to happen every time?

Would there be that many more times??

She continued to chew as she deliberated on her answer.

"Yes and no. I'm near the patio."

Webster indicated he was writing something. Probably something like, "aw, what a shame catch ya later."

The answer instead sent her pulse to the stratosphere.

"Wanted me all to yourself?"

She let out a gust of air and grazed the back of her shaking fingers across her mouth, gaped open from shock.

That one got her straight in the nether regions. No fantasizing needed.

She thought for a moment of what to say back.

Should she flirt? Because he was flirting with her.

He was flirting with her!

What the hell was he thinking!!

He may be a multi-billionaire with a penchant for models, but he was still a dude.

She could swear she did feel a connection. *But don't we all,* Amara thought?

This connection, however, she assumed was intellectual. He didn't seem like the type who would be into brains. But even if he was, headquarters was full of MENSA members so why her?

Are any of them built like you, though, said the black angel on her other shoulder.

Amara grinned at her wicked thought. She did have a phat ass, thank the blessed angels for that.

But... Grayson Davis though??

Her mind replayed all the high-quality candids of him in magazines, wearing blazers, expensive watches, and elegant shades. Arm in arm with tall, leggy blonde twigs with crystal blue eyes. Genetic lottery winners. And never the same one twice. It just didn't add up.

She tried to picture him again in the conference room. An elegant sex magnet, but a calm one. Professional. A fountain of wisdom. He seemed to respect her as an equal.

No. She couldn't flirt. Anything remotely flirty would ruin this, whatever it was. He seemed to be flirting that's true, but no way would she make a fool of herself in case that was a delusion.

The app indicated he was writing something else and she tried to beat him to it.

"I was under the impression I was meeting you here to discuss my future? Was I wrong?"

"I want some of the other team leaders to have a chance to talk to you," he wrote back.

Do what now??

"Why?"

"Just trust me," was all he wrote.

Trust him? For what?

Her heart was in her throat. Surely he must know the effect he was having on her.

Darn you, trust issues, she thought. She was about to do the exact opposite.

Amara gathered her things and made her way to the center of the cafeteria where the Frankentable had formed.

There were about 10 minutes left of lunch, and the herd had been significantly thinned.

"Pull up a chair," he said when she was in view. "Everyone, this is Amara."

She recognized her third-floor supervisor and gave her a sort of stupefied look. She mouthed her a "you're doing great," and Amara nearly teared up.

"Amara has a degree in Literature and... Pedagogy, is that right?"

"Writing and Pedagogy, yes."

"Writing and pedagogy and Amara has expressed to me this morning that she is bored and thinking of quitting."

Oh my God oh my God oh my God.

"But Amara strikes me as very bright and capable, and I would rather not lose her to another company."

OH. MY. GOD.

Without any prompting, the team leaders started asking her questions.

"What is it that you're wanting to do, Amaya," one said, already mispronouncing her name.

"You can call me Amy. Um...I honestly don't know, I'm so sorry."

A few of them looked on with sympathy.

"What were you looking to do when you graduated?"

"Teaching, of course, but at college level. Difficult with only a Master's, but I didn't want to continue with a Ph.D. unless I knew I could commit to the job. I had lots of trouble getting adjunct positions."

"Do you write?" asked another.

"Yes."

"What do you write?"

"Whatever needs writing," Amara answered without hesitation. Grayson exchanged sexy, CEO-esque glances with some at the table.

Was he really about to part the Red Sea for her? They all seemed so composed and she wasn't really sure if she wanted the chance to disappoint him. Amara backtracked.

"But I don't know that I'd call it my passion or anything, I'm just good at it. And I don't know how I'd feel about being forced to do it daily."

"You really *don't* wanna work here, do you," Grayson quipped. Everyone chuckled.

"Oh my gosh, I'm just... this is excruciating." Amara lowered her head with a hand at the bridge of her nose.

The tears were about to start flowing, and she knew it.

Like they did when she came in fifth runner-up in the statewide spelling bee. Like they did when she was forced to do puppetry under duress for her 7th-grade group project. Like they did during her poetry prize ceremony in grad school, when she found out that none of her six submissions made final publication, and she was just invited for participating.

If she was actually good at something rather than just "meh" at everything, maybe *then* she would know what she wanted, and she wouldn't be hoisted into a spotlight, so that everyone could watch her squander an opportunity.

"Breathe, Amara," Grayson eventually said in that deliciously calming voice to which she was slowly becoming addicted. Surprisingly it did calm her nerves, and she raised her head to the ceiling, wiping tears with the corner of her fingertips. The awkwardness was becoming painful, so she just said what she was thinking.

"I'm really sorry that I have no fucking clue what I want to do, and I don't want to take a position I'm not qualified for, only to realize I hate it like everything else, and I definitely don't want to risk disappointing you, so..."

Grayson sat back in his chair, shrinking a little. He had triggered a quarter-life crisis in the poor girl instead of helping her, and he felt rather terrible. The team was quiet and finding interesting things to look at on their phones.

He realized that what had started as a casual, private invitation somehow had become a very formal, very intimidating interview.

The team had, of course, assumed he'd come to headquarters to work non-stop as if he doesn't already. He couldn't very well tell Dale, "can't work now, got a lunch date with the girl from the conference room."

Amara checked her own phone. "Sorry, I'm five minutes late. I have to get back. Sorry."

"Are you aware how much you apologize, Amara?" Grayson said.

Dale gave him a sideways glance.

Sorry, Amara mouthed, eyes tightly shut.

Grayson exhaled a laugh and extended his hand for her to shake. "It was a pleasure to meet you today, Amara."

Amara put a slender hand in his, trying in vain not to be awestruck by his touch.

"I'm never washing this hand," she deadpanned. Only a few at the table snickered. They didn't think much of that one.

Amara slowly gathered her things, and as she turned to hightail it out of there, she heard Grayson behind her.

"Do not quit your job, Amara."

Her back was to them, but he could see she was hiding her face again as she had outside the conference room.

But it was too late.

Grayson Davis had seen her.

CHAPTER 3

* * *

Grayson took his private plane the long distance from Silicon Valley to his penthouse in the Hollywood Hills. It was a 90-minute flight, but with traffic alone would take eight hours to make the same trip by driving. He was eager to get home, take a long shower and relax.

It'd been a long day, but an interesting one, thanks to Amara "Amy" Riley. He knew his staff probably thought he was losing his grip but he could care less about that.

He anticipated an earful from Dale, but there was no need because he knew his old friend well enough to know what he was going to say. Something along the lines of "Dude, what the hell. The company the company blah blah blah."

Grayson couldn't help but see a bit of himself in Amara. He'd always known what he wanted to do, but he knew what it was like trying to survive in an environment where you weren't being challenged.

Before the bipolar misdiagnosis, it had been one of dyslexia, in 2nd grade, when he'd still been unable, or unwilling, to read or write. They put him in special education classes, where he met his first bully. He could fight when pushed far enough, but he preferred carefully crafted insults because they seemed to be more effective. They stuck in people's minds much longer than a fight and often won the war no matter who won the physical battle. He would construct them while at home, commit them to memory and recite them at school whenever the moment struck.

Everyone eventually learned to stay out of the crosshairs of the unapologetic weirdo that was Grayson Davis. His schoolmates collectively breathed a sigh of relief when he dropped out of high school. Columbine had happened the year before, and he struck all of them as school shooter material.

Amara probably wasn't secretly a genius, but she was clearly lost and being pigeon-holed by imbeciles. There had to be a place for her in his company that would allow her to flourish.

He knew he was obsessing about her career choices to keep himself from obsessing about *her*. The chemistry was there and wildly mutual, little did she know. The fact that she had ditched him at lunch as if she'd had better to do.

The fact that she'd admitted to the CEO that she was going to quit and had no "fucking" idea what she was doing in life.

She wasn't out to impress him, he realized. She really just wanted to talk to him. Connect with him. Even if just for a second. And that, for him, was rare. Even more rare, she wasn't desperate. She'd just as soon have taken nothing, rather than to have less than what she was after.

He was sort of developing a crush on her now. It was quaint and unexpected and he liked the feeling, he had to admit. She was completely open yet mysterious. Young and naive but mature and poised. Her name, her smile, her sense of humor. Her walk. Her *talk.*

Maybe he was reading too much into her, but even that was a welcome change. Not since college was he able to be un-jaded about a woman. A black woman! The notion left him feeling very cosmopolitan.

It'd been a few months since his last "relationship" if you want to call it that, and for him, that was a long, long time. Laura Rooney from Melbourne, who was excessively blonde and complained about being bored. A lot. He got the impression she was trying to implicate herself as above it all. She was. Too bad she wasn't very self-aware to boot.

Not that he was really considering *dating* Amara.

But he was, unfortunately, starting to fantasize about her. Because the way she'd reacted to his instant messages in the cafeteria pretty much made that inevitable.

Yes, he had watched her.

It was an entirely unhealthy, creepy stalker habit that he liked to watch people undetected. He guessed it gave him a sense of power that he felt he didn't otherwise possess. The same compulsion got him left back in kindergarten, and his brief stint at the NSA had sent it spiraling out of control.

He'd drifted out into deep water with Amara, however. Because the way she'd devoured her own lip at his words had sent his head reeling.

And then when he'd taken it too far out of greed and was rewarded with her wide-eyed sensuality, it was like taking his first hit of a designer drug.

It was a good thing she'd interrupted his next message with a level-headed response, because had she sent something along the lines of what he saw in her eyes, well. The day would've ended very differently.

Needless to say, he was torn.

He wanted her in ways that conflicted. He certainly didn't want her to quit. He envisioned her leading in some capacity. Capable, generous, bringing out the best in other employees. Smart ideas.

He'd mentor her personally but he knew himself well enough to know that could only end one way. Amara on his private plane, working late hours. Amara unbuttoning her boring white blouse, mumbling fatuous apologies. Little Amara, so worried about disappointing him.

Had she really cried in front of the team like that? He relived the moment in the shower. And was it the result of passion or just anxiety? Either way, she seemed just a little too intense, which was definitely contrary to his libido's agenda.

She seemed kind of... virginal. He'd lost virginity late in life, which either gave him an unconscious bias, or virginity radar, he couldn't quite tell.

If he was right, then she would definitely cling. He hated the sound of that. He welcomed the revolting thought, letting it sway him back toward reason.

But if he ever touched her she'd come apart at the seams, he was sure.

Damn.

He could make her turn to mush. Or would she turn to lioness under his tutelage? He unconsciously let out a groan at the thought. He'd let her dominate.

He snickered to himself and beat his forehead against the travertine tile.

"You need to get laid, dude," he counseled himself.

Next week would be the Malibu party. He'd always had luck at one of Gino's events. Not a woman less than an 8 in a mile radius.

After his shower, he laid in bed trying to convince himself not to check Amara's profile before turning in, but it was no use, he couldn't help himself.

It's not like he'd be at headquarters again anytime soon. He was safe.

When he opened his app, he found that she'd already sent him a message four hours ago. He broke unconsciously into a grin as he read.

"How did you know my name?"

Busted. Is that why his heart rate shot up? He thought for a moment.

"I'm like the Wizard of Oz in that way..." he wrote.

She was online too, so when his response finally came, she replied immediately.

"I've been thinking..."

His grin widened. He was riveted.

"Are you or have you ever been Travis from Quality Control?"

Double busted. What could he do, deny it? The beating in his heart hadn't slowed.

"I'm sure I don't know what you're talking about."

Smooth.

"Aha!" she replied.

He chuckled to himself. What time was it? What was she wearing? No, he couldn't ask that.

"What gave it away?"

She was typing.

"Your voice sounded... familiar."

He couldn't help imagining her saying that in person. Somewhere that wasn't the office. She had no idea what she was doing to him and it took him aback how much he craved it. He responded back to her.

"I knew I should've gone with my British villain accent. Good memory, btw"

"It was very unusual. Unusual things don't happen around there often," she added.

He shook his head. Perhaps she was beyond help. The working world had only begun to eat her soul. He felt lucky there was only ever one thing he cared about, one thing he was good at.

"I feel bad that you hate working at my company."

"Lol I don't hate it."

Grayson continued. *"And I regret that I ambushed you today. Twice. I feel responsible."*

"Best day of my life. Truly."

"I made you cry," he said. Butterflies formed in his gut against his will. Really?? He'd long been over the groupie thing, so what was the deal?

"Lolololol Yes, but then...you touched my hand."

Yikes. Butterflies somewhere else. Perhaps she'd felt something too, but likely for a different reason.

"Washed it yet?"

Her response was quick.

"Nope."

Doing anything else with that hand?

Grayson looked at what he had just written, a boyish grin breaking out on his face, a nimble finger grazing his upper lip.

He was going to erase it, but he let it stand there suspended for a moment. Threatening to alter his life in unending ways.

If he were just a regular guy he could get away with sending it. Then again, if he were a regular guy he'd probably get shot down. He could see Amara was typing.

He thought about how Dale suggested in the early days that they add some way to indicate the other party was typing. Grayson had argued against it, saying something about altering the brain chemistry of every human by decreasing their collective capacity to delay rewards in the pleasure center of the brain. In the end, Dale got his way, and it turned out they were both right. It sent Webster soaring beyond their competitors within months.

Grayson hit the backspace button until his inward confession was no more.

Go to bed, he counseled himself.

"Good night, Amara."

Amara had stopped typing too. He wondered what she'd almost said as he read her simple response.

"Good night."

4

Chapter 4

Amara didn't necessarily think she could single-handedly bring down the company by not working, but she was pretty sure that a person should not be allowed to stare at a blank screen for seven hours and still get paid.

Last week's course of events had a devastating effect on her already dismal work ethic.

She was now two days into her final two weeks' notice.

Her supervisor had called Amara into her office after receiving the parting email, and Amara cried at work for the second time in a week.

"I want to care about your drink order, I really do," Amara sobbed, "but I just don't. I can't do this anymore."

Her supervisor gave her a frown and sighed.

"I don't want you to care about my drink order, Amy. I want you to find your place, and this just isn't it. I know how much you wanted to find it here."

She felt guilty that she wasn't able to stick it out as Grayson Davis had wanted. But she couldn't stay objective about the roller coaster of emotion that she was on, that he had put her on.

He'd given her a taste of what it was like to be desired, in one capacity or another, and the awakening had been so excruciating that she simply could not stack a single other useless piece of paper on top of another. She didn't know what she was going to do, but it couldn't be here, at the scene of the crime.

The eventual conference call with the girls did not exactly help her adjust.

Mya, her roommate, cuddled up with a pillow next to her on the comfortable couch while Amara held the phone in front of both their chins so that Kim could hear. Kim was two time zones away and lounging with a glass of wine while Mya and Amara had just barely survived the rush hour traffic.

"GIRL!" was the only thing Mya could say as Amara ran back the details of the day.

Mya was best friend #1, a ballet dancer who supported herself by doing hair. She'd convinced Amara to move to California with her and currently had more revolving hair clients than she had auditions. Which was a good thing, because Amara was about to make herself available to the industry yet *again*.

"GET OUTTA HERE!" was Kim's only chorus until Amara was done with the last incredible detail.

Best friend #2, Kim, had just finished law school and got hired on at a prestigious company as a corporate lawyer back in Nashville where the girls were all from. Her life was the stuff of Oscar-nominated tragedy and she was a resilient, boisterous, gorgeous, walking miracle.

"And now all I want to do is have his babies," Amara concluded. Kim was laughing but Mya wasn't. She was studying Amara with an expressive look of shock.

"He was flirting with you, Amara!" Mya said soberly.

Mya was the second person to conclude as much that day, but what could it mean beyond a random encounter? People acted as though it were a reason to get her hopes up about something.

"I don't know if he was or not, but —"

"Amara, please staaahp you know guys are constantly on you." Kim warbled through the phone.

"Well for one, dudes hangin' out the passenger side of their best friend's ride don't count and two... I think I would know if I ever caught a white billionaire's attention."

"Really, cuz you did, and you have no idea," said Mya.

"What does the 'billions' have to do with anything, girl men are men. Okay?

They all gotta get it the same way," Kim opined between sips of wine.

"He can afford to have his flown in though," Amara countered.

"I don't know, guys like him are working all the time. And wasn't he like a programming nerd hermit growing up? His social skills are probably nil," Kim suggested.

"Um, no...I definitely got the impression that he is drowning in it."

"Well yeah, bet you don't need social skills when you're a billionaire," Mya shrugged with an exaggerated look of DUH.

"He's like, electric. You should've seen them all in the cafeteria crowded around him like Jesus at the last supper," Amara recounted.

"Girl, Jesus was a loner, so crowds don't mean anything."

"Yeah, he's the boss. He's the boss of the boss. Of course, he can talk about work, but I bet he'd be awkward as hell at a party," Mya continued.

"*I'm* awkward as hell at a party," Amara interjected, "what does all that have to do with anything?"

"I think Mya is trying to suggest that this might be a nerdy match made in swirl heaven, and I might have to agree," Kim's voice lilted. Mya shrieked and clapped her hands as Amara looked on.

"Swirl heaven? Wow. You're both crazy," Amara deadpanned.

"Amara, don't be afraid to want something impossible," Mya counseled soothingly. She was the encourager of the group.

"You are terrible at giving advice, you know that?" Amara shot back with laughter in her voice.

"I mean it, Amara. You always think amazing things can't happen to you, but luck is preparation meeting opportunity, you understand? You got a crazy energy of opportunity swirling around you right now, and the next crazy thing that happens, whatever it is, you just need to say yes."

Amara's mind drifted to all the sexual things Grayson could do to her that she could say yes to.

"And just what is this amazing impossible thing I'm supposed to not be afraid to want? Love? A booty call? A baby daddy?"

"YES!" Kim confirmed all three emphatically.

"Well, anyway it doesn't matter because he only visits headquarters like, less than once a year. I doubt I'll see him again."

"Girl, forget about work, you better be texting him at 3 am," Kim said.

Amara was horrified at the thought.

"No way. The only way I'd ever text him is if he texts me first," Amara lied. "And I'm not gonna hold my breath for that one."

She didn't tell the girls that she'd already sent him a message earlier that day asking how he'd known her name.

Nor did she tell them when, four hours later, he'd answered.

The playful chime that indicated his response nearly sent her into cardiac arrest. It was just like her early days of online chatting and suddenly she was 12 again, racing home after school to chat with men twice her age. At least she thinks they were men.

It was strange territory being forged then, and it was the same for her now. Only this time she didn't have to worry about being assumed to be white and, for some reason, with him she hesitated less than she ever had with anyone.

* * *

From the time Amara had come back from the infamous lunch to now, the third floor had been a buzz. When she put in her notice, strangely the news traveled.

"Isn't this *the* Amy Riley?" they'd whispered in HR.

"She quit her job anyway?? Awkward," they texted to each other.

"Were they screwing?" they wondered at lunch.

"Grayson Davis only dates blondes."

"Yeah, I think he considers brunettes a minority group."

Dale, the COO and Grayson's best and oldest friend, thought it wise to give his best and oldest friend the news over the phone, along with some other choice words so that he could feel him out.

Dale put Grayson on speaker.

"So I thought you should know... your white whale turned in her notice a few days ago."

Odd choice of words, Grayson thought as he said a curse to himself.

"Did she say where she was going?" he asked.

"Grayson..." Dale answered.

"Dale," Grayson answered back.

"What the hell, dude."

"What?"

Dale was silent. Grayson continued.

"I saw something in the girl, and I know you saw it too."

Still more silence.

"She's ballsy and smart. She deserved the full Grayson Davis experience," Grayson defended himself. That response earned him more silence. In his mind, he could see the look Dale was giving him.

"She was in a cubicle black hole doing third-floor inanities," Grayson defended.

"Not every wandering, aimless bleeding heart is you, Grayson," Dale finally said.

"That's not what that was," Grayson protested.

"No you're right, that was something... way less appropriate."

"Oh, come on."

"The fact that you would try and deny it... to me of all people...."

"Name one unprofessional thing I did."

"Okay, how about two? You did your weirdo creeper routine from the corner hallway AND YOU WERE SEXTING HER," Dale announced slowly and loudly from the plush privacy of his office.

Grayson rolled his eyes. "Okay, first of all, no one saw that, and secondly, I was not 'sexting' her that is ridiculous."

Dale wiped his face down with his hand. "I can't believe this conversation exists."

"It's under control, Dale. I was never gonna act on it, and now you'll never have to worry."

"Under control? Have you even stopped to think how the hell I would know whether or not a 2nd tier assistant to a project manager put in her notice?" Dale asked.

"Sorry, I don't spend my days pondering about how you come to know things."

"This little outburst of yours has reverberated through the entire building, Grayson."

"Was it really 'an outburst'?"

"I felt like I was watching Black Swan."

"No pun intended right? Dude, you're racist," Grayson accused.

"Really," Dale sounded uninterested in the assessment.

"Hardcore."

"Look, before you start deflecting to death, I bring it up not because I'm desperate to talk about it, but because you haven't. At all. And that's really fuckin' weird. I don't like to have to guess about where your head is."

"My head is where it's always been," Grayson replied.

Dale ignored the pun. "Well, I have no choice but to believe you. But dude, we really can't afford to have any more incidents like that. The dress code violations are already through the roof when you stop by. We're going to have to start handing out garbage bags the next time."

"Excuse me for taking a personal interest in the professional development of an employee." He continued after a beat. "Honestly, it's pretty sad that our people see it so rarely that they have to resort to rumor mills."

"So you've heard the rumors then?"

"Such as?"

"Such as Amy had to leave because she's secretly carrying your child?" Dale recited.

"Well... that's just ridiculous."

"Is it?"

"Yes, obviously I'd never make someone quit their job because they were pregnant with my child," Grayson quipped.

"You're hilarious."

"Honestly, why would I want her to work at Webster if I wanted to sleep with her? If that were the case, I would've been urging her to quit, not finding her a permanent place in the company. Where I'd have to constantly avoid her so she wouldn't drive me crazy."

After another pregnant pause, Dale began again, his brow wrinkled.

"...Okay, well when you're ready to be honest with me, you know where to find me."

"Dude get over yourself, I don't need to lie about who I decide to be interested in."

"You know I've never judged any of your... choices. Personally, I think it would be great for you to date a real person with actual human qualities and attributes. It might even last longer than one moon cycle."

"I see no reason to fix what isn't broken," Grayson said.

"Well, that's debatable."

"It's been seven years since I saw my first billion with a 'b' dollars. Do you have any idea what that does to a man's libido?"

"Yes I do, I was there."

"A moon cycle is more than adequate. There's not an ounce of settling down in my blood right now. And I will never have to worry about finding someone. Because I am a billionaire."

"You've said that."

"With a 'b'."

For the millionth time, Dale made a futile attempt at introspection.

"And you're gonna share that with just... any old gold digger."

"Dude, we've been over this."

"The old 80/20."

"Exactly. The 20-year old that survives 80-year-old sex with me gets it all."

The 80/20 was Grayson's way of saying he didn't know, and didn't want to talk about it, Dale knew.

"You're a depraved individual," Dale simply said.

"Will I see you in Malibu?" Grayson changed the subject.

"Yeah, if I can survive this ridiculous conversation with you," Dale chided.

"As you were, then. I'm seriously backed up, and I need a wingman."

"Dude, I thought we talked about the plumbing metaphors."

* * *

Amara must've typed "hey" to Grayson Davis a million times in the subsequent two weeks.

She never sent it, only typed it. And then erased it.

As much as she dreamed of Grayson Davis being completely accessible to her, the idea of potentially being a nuisance to him was an unbearable nightmare.

A couple of times she wrote him some pretty long, fanciful sonnets about what that morning meant to her, and his voice and his eyes on her, and his hope, however fleeting, on her.

She erased those too.

Then once she actually wrote that she hated him for what he'd done, making her normal life utterly unbearable. And also how she'd like to lose her virginity to him.

Erased.

It was reckless to do it that way. One knee-jerk pinky to the enter key and she would've been found dead in her room from embarrassment.

But it was a total rush. Cathartic. The only way to cope after dozens of resumes sent out into the ether, only to receive a gaggle of automated replies. Amy Riley's resume wasn't even enough to get a face to face anymore.

Had Amara's time at Webster been one dead-end position too many?

She'd found two jobs that she was particularly excited about. One was an on-air talent position, which was terrifying, but it was a position doing interviews. Press junkets. The prospect thrilled her. She didn't trust she'd be any good in front of a camera, but she knew she would be a killer interviewer. She had no experience, but it wasn't needed. And it paid peanuts. She was overqualified, really.

She'd thought about calling in a favor with Grayson but in the end, the prospect just made her sick. She had access to one of the richest, most influential men in the world, and she was squandering it.

The man had 500 million connects. What were the odds he would be willing to take time out of his insane schedule to call in some rinky-dink favor?

He sort of seemed like that type of guy.

But what if he wasn't?

In the end, she just ended up following up with the job incessantly, until they told her over the phone that the position had been filled.

The other one turned out to be, well, fake let's just say. Hence, the desperate unsent messages.

Besides, knowing that instant messages work two ways, every non-message day that passed chipped away at the confidence he'd tried to instill in her.

The first time was a fluke, she convinced herself. The hours between his response had been unbearable enough, but she'd muddled through. She just had to find out how he knew her. She'd received a satisfactory answer.

At least, it seemed satisfactory at the time.

But then she only had more questions like, did he know her name *before* he'd called as Travis from QC or after? And how had he recognized her? And why hadn't he revealed to any of the team that he had spoken to her once before?

Would he ever talk to her again?

The easiest way to live day to day was never to have to guess again. So, after ten days of torture, she blocked him.

By day 5 of Amara's two weeks' notice, things seemed to settle back to normal. The buzz of Grayson's visit was slowly drowned out by the ocean of minutiae that needed looking after by the human-machine that is Webster.

Amara had gained a few friends through her notoriety, a few brash souls that introduced themselves and had all kinds of questions. The lack of familiar faces reminded her just how large the company was, even though it started as just two friends in Dale's apartment just ten years ago.

Little was known about the very private Dale, the man behind the man behind the company, except that he was the chief operating officer and had been Grayson's best friend growing up. If he was brilliant no one even knew that, though it had to be true to be where he was. He generally walked softly and carried a big stick, which earned Amara's respect on a level par with Grayson's.

So when Amara's supervisor came by her desk with Dale's secretary from the second floor, Amara nearly fainted when she heard the words:

"Mr. Abernathy would like a few words with Amy if you don't need her right now."

"Absolutely."

Amara heard her supervisor reply and all sound morphed as if she was suddenly underwater. It seemed just when she thought she'd survived a current of crazy, here came another to suck her back in. She could deal with one reality or the other, she just didn't know if she could stand all the flux. *Pick a plotline, God,* she thought.

She got up from her seat and didn't dare look in the direction of any of her fellow workers this time. She couldn't feign bewilderment with them any longer. She was being singled out from them for some reason, and she was dreading all the arbitrary awkward farewell sentiments, signed "We'll Miss You" cards, and excuses to eat cake coming her way.

As Amara followed his secretary downstairs, who enjoyed a very large and plush office with elegant oversized double doors, she wondered if she could put, "Sat outside of Dale Abernathy, COO's office door" on her resume, because she knew she was breathing rarefied air, she just didn't quite know why.

"Bring her in," she heard over the loudspeaker ominously. His secretary smiled warmly as if to put her at ease.

"Just go right in, Amy," she said.

Amara walked past her desk and into a large room with floor to ceiling windows, a panoramic view of the Webster offices down below on the first floor.

Dale Abernathy was sitting at his computer looking focused on his work. The youthful appearance of the already rather young COO made him look like a high school student playing pretend at Dad's office. Yet he had the similar gravitas of his best friend.

"Sit down, Amara," he said, taking Grayson's cue and using her full name.

She complied and looked around, wondering what she was doing here and remembering her wise friend's words. *The next crazy thing that happens, whatever it is, just say yes.*

Dale finished up one last thing on his laptop before he turned his attention to Amara and gave her a gracious smile.

"The infamous Amara Riley."

Amara lowered her head and put her hands on her temples.

"Should I ask for an autograph?"

"You wouldn't happen to know what's going on, would you?" Amara quipped.

"I was hoping you could tell me," Dale answered. "I spoke to Grayson about you, and he wants to know what your plans are once you leave here."

"...You can't be serious." Amara wheezed.

"I'm completely serious," he said.

"Dale... can I call you Dale?"

"You can call me an asshole if you want, you technically don't work here anymore."

"Dale is fine... can you please explain to him that I am ordinary and there's nothing special about me?"

"Well, I wouldn't say that, Amara. In fact, I would say you're pretty extraordinary, and I'd venture a guess as to why but... I'd have to see more to know for sure."

"Okay," Amara simply said, waiting to hear the rest.

"You should know, Amara, that the only people that have known Grayson longer than me are his parents. And I have never before seen... what I saw on Monday, with you."

Amara's tortuous ten days had somehow made her bold.

"Did he tell you that we'd talked once before?"

Dale's eyebrows went up. "No, he didn't."

He seemed to genuinely not know. She continued.

"He didn't know it was me, I'm pretty sure. But I don't know, somehow he figured it out."

"He undercover bossed you?"

"About three months ago, yeah."

"Ah. And did... something else happen?" Dale asked tentatively.

Do what now??

"I... no...I don't think so. I don't follow, I'm sorry," Amara stumbled.

"Never mind. It's just... I know you probably didn't notice... well, you couldn't have known, because you'd have to *know* him to know, but..." Dale glanced back at his laptop before closing it, "you had him really, really flustered."

40

Amara felt involuntary heat filling her face. She smiled and then had to splay her fingers in front of her mouth to hide that her lips were trembling. He continued.

"And *because* I know him so well, you can't possibly imagine how very, very amusing this is for me."

Amara turned her head and let out a breathy laugh into her shoulder. Her eyes were glued to the table.

"And no offense, but I'm glad you've made the decision to move on. Although you seem lovely, the workplace is... not where I want to be amused by Grayson, do you know what I mean?"

"Oh my God," Amara said putting her head in her hands and leaning on the desk in front of her.

She wasn't quite catching his drift, because she refused to believe that Grayson fucking Davis was attracted to her in any way, unless she heard it from the man himself. Yet she was reeling at the idea that it may somehow be a very real possibility.

Maybe he just meant... intellectually flustered. What? That doesn't exist.

But... it can't be... the other thing. She was too frightened to ask for clarification.

"I have a proposition for you, Amara. And please... do not feel pressure to do anything you don't want. Feel free to say no."

Whatever it is say yes, she thought.

"Well, before I forget... you never told me your plans after you leave."

"Oh yeah, that. Well, I actually got a callback today from Carolina Bread Company."

"Carolina Bread Company," Dale repeated.

"Yeah."

"Doing what?"

"1st shift baker."

Dale slowly reclined back in his swiveling chair.

"1st shift. Isn't that like... three in the morning?"

"Yeah. I'm gonna knead dough while it's dark, and hopefully catch the sunrise and think about what direction I want my life to go in."

Dale thought it best not to comment. "When do you start? Monday?"

"Well, I have one more week here, and then I thought maybe I'd take another week, just to, you know, sleep in as much as I can before—"

"You know what, stop. Because I literally can't listen to any more," his voice went upward as though he were asking a question.

Amara laughed a bit as she replied, "Okay."

"Would you like to make a quick thousand dollars?" he suddenly said.

One month of her portion of the rent and utilities.

She could have an extra two weeks to find something a little more awesome. Four before she had to really start panicking.

Whatever it is, say yes.

"Is this making of one thousand dollars... sexual in some way?" Amara inquired, as a joke.

Dale cocked his head to one side as though thinking. "Not...directly."

Oh, he was serious?!

Amara made a face.

"Okay, let me start over..." Dale said with a wave of his hand. "Do you want to go to a party?"

5

Chapter 5

By the time Grayson arrived in Malibu, the party was in full swing. Even though the sun had barely commenced setting, streaking the sky with purple. He was clean-shaven and wearing an oatmeal-colored linen suit that was light and airy and draped him beautifully.

Not even five minutes in he was looking at his watch. He hadn't heard a thing from Dale yet, which was unusual. He was a billionaire, but he relied on his wingman, pathetic as it seemed to him to admit that.

He went to the bar that was on a deck overlooking the beach. The decor was sleek to match the profile level of all the attendees. Clean and modern with a black and white scheme, the strings of outdoor lights and other rustic touches there to add a degree of casual intimacy to the atmosphere. The level of celebrity there was excessive enough to shrink the entertainment world down to its actual size. Peppered among that crowd were beautiful plastic blonde nobodies, looking to snag a somebody. No one was bothering him.

Yet.

Today though he was off his game and he could feel it.

Was he even in the mood? He was most definitely overdue, but he couldn't place the source of the frustration.

Surely this isn't her *doing,* he said to himself.

But then, when he thought of Amara, he felt the sudden flow of blood beyond his belt, and he knew he had a serious, serious problem.

After their online chat, he'd decided to try and truly scrap this Amara thing.

He couldn't sit around messaging her like a pedo. Besides, what would he say, what could he say that wouldn't cause her to leap to conclusions?

Once it seemed like she was beating him to the punch and typing him something, but she must've changed her mind because nothing was ever sent.

Probably for the best.

Then the knowledge that she was now an ex-employee and free to be openly pursued had only caused anxiety to bubble up in him, one that he instinctively knew to heed. It would be exchanging one kind of freedom to lose another. He thought about asking her where she was going, trying to help her in some way. He didn't know why he felt responsible for her at all, but he did.

Then he thought surely she must be a Rules girl because last night he discovered that she'd up and blocked him.

Had she meant to send his hunting instincts into overdrive? Because he nearly made it his life's ambition to make her beg for it.

And that was scary. Because any woman that could make him consider putting aside his rationale was dangerous indeed.

Yet part of him was in denial because he was pretty confident that Amara was incapable of sexcapades-level mind games.

He knew for a fact that Amara was painfully innocent and loyal, and deep down he was a stubborn, cantankerous smartass, impossible to live with.

She deserved a relationship, but he certainly wouldn't be the one to foist a trauma like that on her. He would make a terrible boyfriend. A terrible husband. Terrible dad. So why bother? It was the basis for his 80/20 compromise.

Grayson never considered having children. Working for the NSA had made him cynical about the world he ultimately couldn't help trying to improve.

Why bring kids into this world and give them tons of money until they're useless, ultimately adding to the misery? He made a great fearless leader, but romance-wise he could never unleash himself on a girl like Amara Riley. His conscience wouldn't allow it. Better to leave her to her overblown perceptions than to—

"There he is," Dale's familiar drawl interrupted his thoughts.

"It's about time," Grayson began. "I was starting to—"

Grayson turned from the bar, and his heart nearly jumped out of his chest. There standing before him was Amara, fucking, Riley.

Her locs were unleashed from their demure updo she maintained in the office and were now cascading down her bare shoulders as they did in her Webster profile pictures. She was wearing a simple black halter top dress and, sweet mother of mercy her cleavage... he nervously forced his eyes to meet hers. Was she even wearing makeup?

He hoped he was managing a smile. A slender bronze arm was tightly coiled around Dale's dress shirt sleeve, and he could tell she was nervous because she was holding on to Dale for dear life...

She was holding on to Dale...

Amara suddenly turned her head to one side, behind Dale's shoulder, revealing that beautiful ligament in her neck that was more pronounced in certain women when they turned. Grayson's pulse quickened as he studied the two of them.

What the fuck was going on?

"Grayson... how's the party buddy?" Dale started as if trying to pretend something wasn't happening when it was. He gently shrugged the shoulder Amara was hiding behind and she faced forward, smiling shyly and looking around.

"You remember Amara," Dale began again since Grayson seemed to be speechless.

"How could I forget," Grayson managed smoothly. "Are you...did you guys—"

"I flew her in this afternoon. Turns out we have quite a few things in common," Dale continued, looking into Amara's eyes. Amara took her free hand and moved it to her mouth. She made a jerking movement forward with her head, as though summoning her locs to cover the side of her face, and they complied, shielding her expression from Grayson like a beaded curtain.

"You're not... you're cool with it right?" Dale said almost daring him to find fault with it.

Grayson was lost in a battle fending off despair but didn't let it show. He began to say "of course," but he could only manage a laugh and a slow shaking of his head as he eyed the two of them.

Dale wasn't quite sure if he was taking the bait, so he went on to make sure.

"I just figured, you know after our conversation and all and.... Now she's not technically an employee so—"

"It's fine, Dale. Just, leave it. You're making Amara uncomfortable."

Dale stared back at him blankly for a long while.

Grayson looked over at Amara who was also staring at him with two giant, endlessly dark orbs. She looked a bit apologetic.

Was he missing something else? Was something else coming??

Dale's poker face dissolved into an ever-increasing satisfied smile, and he began that sickening silent chuckle of his, that had often caused physical confrontations between them in adolescence.

"Oh my gosh... that was horrible, Dale," Amara broke in sweetly in Dale's direction.

They'd clearly already had a rapport. Hot jealousy slinked around Grayson's middle and choked his lungs.

"No, that was... worth seven years of Christmas bonuses." Dale laughed outwardly this time, wrapping an arm around Grayson's shoulders, his laughter increasing with every humorless second Grayson was eyeing him. Grayson looked as though he could easily punch him, and for some reason it only made Dale crack up even more.

Amara could clearly see the years between them now, and it was a priceless moment. Suddenly they were not two of the wealthiest men in the world, just two bros at a party engaged in the numbskull things bros did.

Dale turned to Amara, grabbed her wrist with one hand and reached into his jacket pocket with the other. A wad of cash emerged, and he put it in her open hand.

"I can't take this blood money," Amara whined.

"Take it," Dale laughingly groaned. "Best money I've ever spent." He put his hand on each of their backs, standing between them and shoved. "Go be young, you two."

They bumped into each other slightly when Dale did that, shattering the awkward workplace tension between them. A new kind of tension formed to take its place.

As they lazily drew apart again, Amara grabbed his arm and drew herself close to it. He could feel the warm tenderness of her breast through his suit jacket, painfully aware of the bra she was not wearing. One mere layer of clothing away from being completely naked— was she wearing underwear? He was theorizing what kind when she spoke.

"You have to know that this was entirely his idea. I only agreed because Dale assured me you would think it was hilarious."

"He just said that so you'd do it," Grayson answered flatly.

"I feel so used!" Amara laughed.

Her laughter softened him. He changed the subject. "Your hair looks—"

"Looks like worms?" Amara volunteered.

"What? No. I was gonna say you look different when it's down."

"Oh," she said, somewhat surprised. "Different good?"

He nodded sweetly, and her wobbling legs were no closer to recovering.

"But also it looks like worms?" she assumed.

"Hear that a lot, do you?" he inquired.

"Once a week, at least."

"Even in the city?" he wondered. "Where do you live?"

"Palo Alto."

"Ah," he said as if that explained things. "I'm paying you well enough to live there?" he quipped.

"Not even, no offense," she said. He took none, and she continued as they walked.

"Mya's aunt owns the house. She's had it for like, thirty years. Mya's my roommate. We wanted to be in Oakland, but we basically moved here with nothing, so it would've been stupid not to take her aunt's offer. It's much cheaper, even with the hellish commute."

"Well, I think it's beautiful," he said, returning the subject to her hair.

"Thanks," she said, as her eyes went skyward.

He smiled. "So...what do you think?"

"About what?"

"The party."

"...Meh," Amara simply said sarcastically.

"Not impressed?" He grinned.

"Five of my adolescent obsessions are here," she replied.

"Five?"

"At least five, yes."

He looked down at her as they walked arm in arm and frankly, was overwhelmed.

She smelled floral but he couldn't quite place it. Lavender? Vanilla? He was close enough to her bare shoulders to kiss them. She was wearing hoop earrings and a modest gold necklace with a cross. So she did wear jewelry.

The top half of her back was exposed and either that was her ass, or she was smuggling something. The drape of her dress accentuated the drama of her figure and her graceful movements that were almost feline. The sight of so much of her glowing brown skin nearly hypnotized him. She literally made his mouth water.

"You look gorgeous," he finally said.

This. is. happening, she thought.

She was wearing her roommate's dress, the fanciest thing between them, arm in arm with *him*, and he was saying all the right things.

"I feel underdressed," she confessed.

"You probably spent a fraction of what these women spent on their outfits, but I can't take my eyes off you."

Holy hell! *This guy is trying to get laid,* she thought.

Not that her body knew the difference, because she could feel it reacting to his every word and movement with all kinds of zings and spontaneous bursts.

Mya and Kim had tried to coach her as much as they could in 2 hours.

"He's going to say whatever he needs to say to sleep with you," Kim predicted.

"He literally doesn't need to say anything," Amara protested.

"DO NOT give it up to him on the first night, Amara! Unless you never want to see him again," Mya said.

Kim was a little more pragmatic.

"Girl, GET IT. And try to get pregnant."

Amara snapped herself back to the present.

"Well, since this dress is borrowed, I'd say you're right, Mr. Davis," she answered.

"Amara... you can call me Grayson, you know that."

"People are looking at me, Grayson."

The sound of his name coming out of her wide feminine mouth triggered a pang of hunger he'd never known before, to hear his name out of her again at least one million more times, and in all its infinite combinations.

"They're trying to figure out who you are and why you're with me," he finally said.

"And who am I?" she smoothly countered.

"Who do you want to be?" he answered back, not to be outdone.

"Hmmm..." she replied.

Your next meal, she thought in her head. She was so achingly close to him, and only after a few minutes she was beginning to get used to it.

She smiled and looked away at something, anything to keep her soul inside her body. She surveyed the plum-colored sunset, marveling. "God, it's beautiful here."

Grayson watched her watching the sunset and studied her expression.

She was taking it in. This was not her life, and he knew she was counting the hours when she would have to return to it.

He had done the same thing at her age. It had driven him to live among this world, but he got the distinct feeling Amara had no intentions of counting herself a part of it.

"Do you want to meet them?" he suddenly said.

"Who?"

"Your adolescent obsessions."

Amara lit up, slightly apprehensive, and then a heart-melting smile. "Yes, I think I would."

Grayson didn't do a lot of mingling, and he'd built up quite a mystique from the practice. He enjoyed little anonymity and relished it when he could get the chance to blend into a crowd. Even if someone was ignorant enough not to know they were in a room with the man responsible for their life's greatest modern distraction, he was often mistaken for some handsome leading man or another, and many times had the unfortunate task of being grilled by strangers to tell them who he was.

But to observe Amara's doe-eyed excitement, Grayson could make an exception.

Grayson and Amara made the rounds, and everyone she met was warm and spoke cordially to her. Amara was her unassumingly delightful self, a pitch-perfect blend of reverent and respectful. A few times she was indeed asked what or where they knew her from, and each time she had replied, "I'm nobody," quickly turning the conversation back to them with some intriguing, genuine question about their work or their process. Her fascination was fascinating, and she pulled some great industry stories out of them while they were loose with liquor and the abandon that came with a safe place of peers.

The party buzzed as Amara reminded her heroes of their prior greatness. Everyone loved it, especially the DJ who called her on the platform to play a request. She, of course, picked the perfect 90's throwback song that sent the party into the stratosphere where it stayed for the rest of the night.

As the evening wore on, Grayson's touch had moved from friendly to flirty to possessive. Amara was aware of each transition. That and the overall surreal nature of the night kept her body on high alert. She was a potent cocktail of anxious, turned on, and completely alive. Grayson handed her a flute of champagne, and they found a gorgeous, white satin draped cabana near the beach. It was one of three others facing a large infinity pool where there were a few swimmers, but mostly everyone was congregated along the edge sipping drinks, which struck Amara as a bit dangerous.

"I can't believe I just met Clarisse Brooke and Noah Taylor."

"Pretty amazing," Grayson admitted.

"They are totally hot together and beautiful. I want them to adopt me."

A random group of people was eyeing them, and Grayson raised his glass to acknowledge them. They did the same.

"So, it seems you were right. Perhaps I have missed my calling," Amara began.

"What's that?" Grayson asked, looking as though he would kiss her.

"I'm not sure how to get paid for it, but it involves going to celebrity parties and generally being awesome," she answered, not looking at him.

"You're good at schmoozing; I'll give you that."

"The secret is just to pretend like you're dreaming," she revealed. "There's a lot of interesting people here."

"Including yourself."

Amara ignored his comment as she took a sip.

"So where is this Palm Hotel I'm supposed to be staying at?"

"Look behind you."

Amara's mouth gaped open "...Holy shit."

"What, did you think Dale would put you up at the Beaver Lodge Truck Stop?"

"Sort of, I mean he already gave me a thousand dollars."

Grayson laughed. "You're drinking a thousand dollars."

She took another sip. "Funny, it doesn't taste like my first car," Amara replied.

"You haven't spent that much time around the affluent have you?"

"The truly affluent are only those who do not want more than they have," Amara quoted.

"Erich Fromm," he cited, inching a single slender digit down her bare shoulder.

Amara shuddered. She took in a sharp breath as she looked past him, hiding a trembling smile.

As she tried and failed to hide her reaction to him, he got even more of the sense that she was horribly inexperienced. That perhaps her mind had been sharpened to within an inch of its life, and in all that schooling she'd left her body behind.

"It's a quote from one of your SPEC conferences," Amara finally said when she was composed enough.

Grayson stood and held out his hand for her to take.

"Where are we going?"

"Just for a walk. It's a beautiful night."

They walked arm in arm wordlessly on the beach in the direction of the high rise hotel. The ocean was barely lit by moonlight and distant tiki lamps. The crashing waves were unusually loud.

"I've been here a few years now, and I never go to the beach."

"Never?"

"Well...more than once, less than thrice."

"You're a virgin aren't you, Amara," Grayson suddenly said.

Amara gave him an eye roll and looked out at the water as though it were endlessly fascinating. "Is it that obvious?"

"Only if you're paying attention," he said. "But I would expect nothing less from you," he continued, smiling. "Saving yourself for the man of your dreams, somewhere out there in the world, the only man that would ever make you feel like a woman."

He was saying it not only in jest but also with the clear indication that he was not nor would ever strive to be that man.

Oh.

The illusion of the night shattered around her with great force, and her heart was pierced with one of the shards. Even with all her fail-safes in place, hope had slipped through her armor, and she was bleeding between its plates.

She smiled through it.

"You're actually incorrect, Grayson Davis, but please, keep trying and failing to read me, it's starting to become amusing."

He stared at her and smiled, the two continued walking.

"It seems I've hit a nerve," he said.

"Not at all," Amara lied. "I just find it funny when guys assume that my lack of experience is a conscious choice. Like I have a gentleman caller waiting list."

"Surely, I can't be your first gentleman caller," he replied.

"No, not the first. But by far the best."

"Don't talk like that," he insisted as they walked.

"Like what?"

"Like... I'm a catch," he said sounding mystified.

"Umm... you are," she replied, mimicking his mystified tone.

"No, I'm not. I don't do relationships because I'm no good with them."

"Why, what happened?" Amara queried.

"Nothing. And it never will," he said.

"Well if you've never had one, how do you know?"

"Isn't there something in your life you don't need to try to know that you'd be terrible at it?"

"Pretty sure I'll be terrible at sex, but like anything else, I'll get better with practice."

Was she baiting him? Flirty little Amara.

"The thought of you being terrible at sex is endearing. Failing at love is not."

Amara was silent, and he continued.

"I'm enthralled with women," he said, "but I can only give them what they want, not what they need."

"That sounds... kind of sad," Amara replied.

"Well that's where you and I differ because it works for me," he asserted, convinced. "If Dale hadn't brought you here I'd probably be elbow deep in a random blonde right now."

"Gross," Amara deadpanned.

"Well, it's true. I should be shattering your illusion of me, not encouraging it."

"I'm under no illusions," she informed him, the breeze subtly blowing her hair.

"Aren't you?"

"You're a playboy, I get that. Most people know that."

Grayson never thought of himself as such. Sex was a need to be fulfilled. And a habit was formed typically after 21 days. So he had to change them out every few weeks, naturally. With periods of solitude in between to, you know, recharge. Women were generally very tiring to him. Like kryptonite he couldn't resist.

But he had very few one night stands. One night certainly wouldn't be enough with Amara, whom he was starting to realize he would never have.

"Not a playboy, just a pragmatist," he corrected.

"Don't you want love?" Amara probed.

Grayson merely shrugged. He tried to remember the last time anyone had asked him that. Dale had asked in a roundabout way. It was the only thing he'd ever wanted, but he'd learned to stop letting that desire rule his life. It was what drove him to fits of blackout rage in his youth, drove him to spiraling depressions that didn't seem to plague other children, what kept him choking down antipsychotic pills for years, and what made him hide them under his tongue years later. The desire for love practically killed him.

"I imagine if I were in your shoes, I'd give up on the idea of anyone loving me for me too," she continued.

Grayson's heart skipped a beat and couldn't seem to recover.

Had she known about his past?

What did she and Dale talk about on the way there?

Did he tell her about the relentless bullying and isolation and the crippling hopelessness it caused? Did he tell her about that macabre Christmas, when his cries for help culminated in what was to be his final grand gesture?

He waited for her elaborate.

When she didn't, he prompted her.

"Why do you say that?"

"Because... you're a billionaire?" Amara said as though she assumed it was obvious.

Oh right, the money.

He smiled, "I've long given up on the idea of permanent companionship, before the money, but yes, it certainly doesn't help."

Amara looked at him then, square in the eyes as though she'd had an epiphany.

She wasn't shy anymore, and she had that same look she'd had in the conference room, and it made him feel the same way.

"I have a very wicked, very naughty idea, Grayson Davis."

"Those are my favorite," he smiled.

"Let me be your gold digger."

6

Chapter 6

G rayson laughed out loud at her words, but Amara didn't.

"You're serious?" he grinned.

"I am totally, 100%, mega balls serious," Amara said, her brow furrowed at the growing sense of brilliance at her own plan.

"Oh, geez..." he groaned increasingly with a lowered head as she spoke.

His out and out refusal was conspicuously absent. He seemed a little dejected at her words, as though disappointed in the shallow gesture.

Was she shallow? She honestly didn't know, she'd never been given the opportunity. She put it out of her mind for the time being. He was missing the big picture, here.

"Let me dig your gold, bro!" Amara slowly exclaimed. She launched into an elevator pitch. "You don't do relationships, but you totally like me and you know it, I'm wicked smart, I'm fun, I'm super low-maintenance, I *love* free food... c'mon dude, this is like, a no-brainer."

He shook his head as he chuckled. "Amara, that's... you're... wow."

She cocked her head at his non-response as she looked at him with complete confidence, her tongue behind her teeth as though her wheels were turning. He couldn't pretend that it wasn't adorable to watch her wheels turn. After awhile a girlish, somewhat cocky grin emerged on her lips.

"What?" he smiled.

"I'm waiting for an answer," she shrugged.

He hesitated as he looked out at the beach, suddenly feeling shy.

Her naive air was lulling him into a false sense of security. What's the harm in entertaining the thought?

The idea of Amara being his next mistress delighted him, it's true. The mere thought of her had made him want to take a vacation. He'd put off having one on no less than four occasions, and now he suddenly couldn't think of a better way to spend his time. Three weeks of Amara in his bed, spoiling her completely rotten... better make it four.

But he couldn't dance around the obvious. His stomach lurched.

"You do realize that gold-digging typically involves sex," he broke the news.

"Yes, I'm... fully aware."

"Amara... I can't take your virginity."

"Why not? Someone has to. You know you want to. I'm pretty sure you know that *I* want you to," she said frankly.

"I do," he admitted, without clarifying to which statement. Amara was all business now and she wasn't bluffing. She continued flippantly.

"You know... now that I'm thinking about it, I think I'm gonna need a lump sum."

"Amara..."

"That should keep everyone off my back for a good long time while I figure out my life."

"I haven't even agreed to this," Grayson interrupted.

"I mean affairs are nice and all," Amara continued as though he hadn't said anything, "but if I'm going to grow accustomed to a certain lifestyle... I'm not going to want to get up and knead bread at 3 in the morning afterward."

Grayson's brow furrowed. "You lost me."

"You didn't hear? I got a job at Carolina Bread Company."

Grayson couldn't help the wide grin spreading across his face. "You're leaving Webster to go bake bread?"

"I'm leaving Webster because I couldn't properly function at all after your visit, and also I get to eat all the bread and pastries I want."

"Amara—"

"So technically this is your fault, and you owe me."

Grayson sighed and craned his neck toward the moon. He was seriously considering her offer and he felt as though at any moment the police would be swooping in on all sides to arrest him.

"How much..." he reluctantly asked, still looking up.

"...A million dollars?" Amara ventured, entirely unsure of the going rate of virginity as well as her own ability to negotiate.

"I'm relieved to see how terrible you are at this," he replied.

"I mean, I know it's a lot—"

"It's not," he simply said.

Damn!

Amara didn't falter. "All the more reason to take the deal then. It's a bargain."

"Amara!"

"Grayson!"

"This is madness."

"It's not, it's pragmatic, like you said, right? How long are we talking, a few months?"

"...More like a few weeks."

Oh.

The confession stung like falling into a cold lake but there it was, and she was starting to get the gist.

Sex was a heartbreaking business and she hadn't even begun in earnest. She was glad to be coming away with a sizeable consolation prize then, and now in much less time than she anticipated.

She suddenly felt ridiculously lucky. She was about to be richer than anyone she knew and it was all due to her hot bod. She found herself confronting an age-old truth and thought about all the women that had come and gone. She wondered if they'd been fed a whole load of bull before they managed to confront the same truth.

Likely not.

"Maybe I should make it whatever would net me a million *after* taxes. Also, maybe there should be some sort of clause where I can pay off my student loans."

"A clause."

"Yeah. I mean, I wouldn't be surprised if you would be able to write this off as a charitable contribution."

"I would pay off all your student loans right now just to see *one* of your boobs," he joked.

Amara looked at him very seriously and he thought she was offended, but then she said, "Oh my God... *this is* my calling."

"I'm just kidding you, Amara," he laughed.

"No you weren't, and honestly, I would enjoy showing you my boobs, almost as much as I would enjoy seeing my student loan balance at zero."

"It's a much better feeling when you can earn it on your own."

"Who says I can't?" Amara said provocatively.

Jeez, maybe this was her calling.

"Look, Amara... I see what you're trying to accomplish, I do. And, maybe I respect it in some way. I won't sit here and pretend to be a better man than I am. I really, really... really want to take the deal. I've spent more money on things so ridiculous I'm embarrassed to admit them."

"I sense there's a 'but' coming."

"But... there's no amount of money that will keep you from falling in love with me."

Grayson Davis was in front of her, using the words "love" and "falling" and "me." And "with."

The words were so vulnerable in her that she thought she'd just as soon die rather than to say them, yet he offered them freely. Her armor was useless it seemed because he was seeing right through her.

"I'm in love with you anyway, only right now I have nothing," she flatly stated.

"You don't even know what you're talking about," he responded gruffly. "Love, virginity, a million dollars, they're all just concepts to you. You have no idea..." his voice trailed off. "Let's say I agree to this thing. When it's over, for you, the pain will likely be excruciating."

He was right. Amara had very little idea what he could be talking about. In her mind, heartbreak could only happen when it was sudden and unplanned.

"Bet I can handle it," she teased. Another wicked smile.

His mind refused to be turned on by the sophomoric response, but his body only laughed in defiance.

He continued, "That's not what I mean, and you know it. You're asking me to be the one to inflict one of the greatest miseries to befall the human heart on you, and you want me to pay you afterwards."

"Quid pro quo, it's only fair," she answered. He still looked apprehensive. Amara tried a different approach.

"Think of it as an education for me, then. Do you wanna know what the last guy who hit on me told me?"

"Not really," he replied honestly.

"He said, 'If you're looking for a stud, I got the *std*, all I need is '*u*.'"

"That's actually... pretty good," he chuckled.

"Save me, Grayson!" she said, grabbing a loose hold of his lapel as if crazed. "If you think I'd have better luck out there, than here with you, then you need to check your privilege."

Grayson laughed aloud again. He couldn't remember the last time he had, and now he was laughing incessantly like he'd had one too many.

"If someone told me that Amara Riley would be at this party propositioning me tonight, I would've told them to pinch me because I was dreaming."

Amara closed the deal, though she knew it was already in the bag.

She let go of his blazer and reached up on tiptoes to put her arms around his neck, though she was tall enough that she barely needed to strain to span his 6'2" height.

She underestimated what the closeness would do to her, but she continued undaunted.

"Take me to parties so I can charm all your snooty friends and they can be all, 'she's so articulate.'"

"Because rich people are unapologetically the worst?" he grinned.

"Wine me, dine me... sixty-nine me," she said, her eyes widening at "sixty-nine."

Yikes. He fought back a few of the mental images.

"You're such a virgin," he said hopelessly.

"Do we have a deal or not, Davis?" she said. He found her faux assertiveness an irresistible challenge.

His hands surveyed her waist for a long moment as he looked down at her full lips. One hand moved to caress her jawline and the nape of her neck, where he could feel her pulse was racing. The hair at the back was softer and lighter than he imagined it. He brushed her long locs to one side exposing her neck and kissed, as though he were a vampire moving in to bite. Her hands moved from around his neck to his shoulders, and she held on for dear life as he teased, lighting up every synapse she had.

He brushed his lips up against her ear, licking and biting. "What room are you in?" he asked quietly.

* * *

The Palm hotel was all white quartz and high ceilings, with deceptively comfortable tufted leather sectionals and chaises, gathered around a white stacked stone feature wall that was also a fireplace. When they arrived arm in arm, they were surprised to see that a portion of the party had moved to the lobby, and the scene was surreal.

A very popular if not forgettable singer was at the piano, and Amara was surprised to see that she could actually play. An older gentleman she recognized as Jerry Stone who was one of Clarisse Brooke's musical directors, the female half of the greatest music couple this century. He was lounging around with artist/producer friggin Pharaoh Stewart singing riffs and runs as the forgettable singer played.

Their large entourage was not quite as respectful. They were blowing smoke in the non-smoking hotel, and seemed to be as new to this level of luxury as Amara was. The air in the hotel was that of discomfort and disruption, but it was overlooked for the sake of the general awesomeness of the sight. They'd kept it to a dull roar, and anyone there that weekend had known about the party and expected as much. They seemed to know they were immune to reproach.

"Amaraaah," Pharaoh sang as she walked in.

Whaaat! She smiled and waved.

"Player play-ah!" One of them said to Grayson as he walked past, the implication not lost on either of them. Grayson didn't seem to know him, but that didn't stop the comment. It was 2am at a celebrity-filled Malibu beach party, after all.

"Gentleman, ladies," Grayson replied cordially. For the first time, Amara could mark the distinction between the man and his image.

"Grayson Davis takin' a walk on the wild side?!" the musical director said, an old interracial relationship reference from the 70's. He reminded her of one of her uncles. Part of her wanted to stay in the lobby and listen to him crack jokes. The singer at the piano seemed to glance at her with a look of jealousy.

"Get that money, girl," said one from the entourage.

She felt Grayson tense under her arm and some of the people that'd met her earlier gave the random onlooker a groaning reprimand.

They were almost at the elevators when Amara unexpectedly stopped and turned to them, piping up in all her stereotypical black glory saying, "Excuse you, I'll have you know that I have a Master's degree from Beaumont University in Writing and Pedagogy, okay, thank you I am not a prostitute."

"Tell 'em girl, get em!" her new best friend Pharaoh egged on. Another person whooped at the elaborate description of her anomalous degree. Everyone was quiet for a beat and she couldn't pass up the opening.

"He *is* about to get it though, so ya'll enjoy the rest of your evening," Amara said.

The room erupted like a bomb went off before she could get the whole punchline out, and when she turned around Grayson had a smile glowing like embers under his disapproving look.

They got into the elevator wordlessly. Grayson pushed her floor and they both watched as the numbers ascended. After a moment, she finally spoke.

"I take it you don't approve of my outburst?" she deduced.

"You sure your calling isn't stand up?" he replied.

"I just made one of my faves die laughing, and you're not going to take that away from me."

"They don't need to know what we're doing."

"They already know. Dale seemed to know the nature of our relationship before you did."

Relationship?

"This isn't a relationship, it's a transaction," he corrected.

"Semantics."

"The more you stick to the semantics the better off you'll be."

"Would you relax? I'm not gonna catch feelings and stalk you afterward if that's what you're worried about."

"You already have, according to you."

She sighed loudly, "I promise not to catch *further* feelings or stalk you afterward, and I absolve you of any responsibility and/or wrongdoing."

Grayson was quiet and seemed satisfied. After a moment she continued.

"Now can you please just be your sexy self and make me feel what I felt on the beach again?" she asked sweetly. A stray loc fell across her face as she cocked her head to the side.

He looked at her and flashed a smile that spiked her temperature. His eyes drew to the floor as though suddenly shy.

"I'm just dropping you off tonight," he said.

"What? Why?" Amara asked urgently.

More smiles. "It's late and, honestly I'm tired, and you deserve to have time to think about this first. Alone."

She wanted to roll her eyes but he was being sensible, she knew. It was chivalrous in a weird way, but nevertheless pointless. Once her mind was made up she could never change it.

"How long do I have," she said.

"We'll spend the day tomorrow," he replied.

His words exploded warm joy along the highways of her heart.

"I'll give you until tomorrow evening."

True to his word he dropped her off without so much as a goodnight kiss. She closed the door behind her, looked around at her ridiculous room— was that her luggage?— and paced it a few times cursing and praying and generally freaking out.

She couldn't help diving backward onto the large plush bed, so comfortable that she lamented the fact that there was no way she was falling asleep anytime soon. She looked at the clock— almost 3 am. She desperately needed to call the girls. It was late but, they would have to deal. It was almost time for Kim to be up for work in Nashville, so she picked up her phone. Kim would be excited.

Mya... less so.

"What...the actual fuck, Amara," Mya said as though wide awake.

"Girl, she got BILLS, THAT'S what the fuck," Kim defended. "Our girl is about to be a *millionaire*. This is some Jane Austen shit."

Amara threw her head back laughing at the two of them, at her situation.

"Jane Austen? Was that also a slave's name that I don't know about, because this right here is the fuckin' Antebellum South." Mya sniped.

Kim rolled her eyes and sighed exaggeratedly, "I don't remember any slaves breaking a million for some poontang," Kim argued.

"Same shit, different era," Mya warned.

"There you go with your atrocity porn again Mya," Kim retorted.

Amara tensed on Mya's behalf.

"Sorry, but that afro-centric high horse mess is played *out*," Kim continued. "The world has changed, and if you ask me, it's even more a matter of survival now than it was then. I was more mad at Amara for insisting on that weak ass degree. And then she *doubled down* on the shit, and got a second one."

Amara laughed, breaking up the tension.

"At least she can pay her bills," Kim lectured. Mya knew Kim well enough to know it wasn't a dig directed at her. "It's not a billion, but as smart as she is, I know she can multiply it and we're gonna help her. She's set for life."

"She's SELLING HER BODY!" Mya exclaimed.

"To a fine ass man who respects her!" Kim preached.

"What kind of man is he that he would even allow her to do this dumb shit? That tells me more about him than anything," Mya retorted.

"Girl, miss me with all that, everybody here is *grown*. He made it clear he's not here for love— no illusions. You know how rare that is just to get honesty out of a man?? It's not happily ever after but hell, this is the next best thing, if not *the* best." Kim was making Amara feel like a genius.

"I knew you'd approve, Kim," Amara broke in.

Kim continued as though she hadn't heard. "And none of y'all have a mom who's strung out and on the street, so if anyone should be mad, it's me— and I'm NOT. This ain't even *close* to the same thing as that."

Amara was silent. Kim's response seemed to temper Mya's emotions.

Mya's voice was level as she confessed, "Maybe you're right Kim, and it'll be perfectly fine but... it's just not what I wanted for you, Amara. You deserve better. You deserve love."

She had love, at least on her end. Wasn't that going to be good enough? Would he love her in time?

Maybe it was a bad idea but she saw no other recourse. She fought back a threatening drizzle of tears.

"You were the one that told me whatever crazy thing happens just say yes!"

"And you pick now to listen to me!!" Mya argued.

"Well, you were right! Girl, those dead-end jobs were killing me, but I trudged through them so I wouldn't leave you out in the lurch. I'm not a lawyer like Kim, I'm not a dancer like you. I just don't have the kind of talent that anyone cares about. But now I've found it out here, and you know what it is? I attract billionaires."

"Amara...."

"I made my half of the rent and utilities for the month in *seconds*, Mya. Just helping Dale with a joke. And now I've made a deal with the man of my dreams, and it's so good that I'll never have to make another one."

"Which reminds me, Amara, let me draw you up a contract," Kim interjected.

"Ugh, I cannot believe we are having this conversation." Mya sounded genuinely concerned.

"I don't know, Kim. I don't want to like, scare him off with a bunch of legalese," Amara argued.

"If he gives you a buncha shit about protecting yourself, then you should *definitely* back out," Mya insisted. "There's no virtue in being naive about it, if you're gonna do it."

"I gotta agree with my girl on that one," Kim said.

Amara's guts fluttered and she sighed. "Fine."

Whatever this was, it was definitely *not* Jane Austen shit.

"Have you even thought about *after* he's done using you?" Mya suddenly offered.

"Nope," Amara answered glibly. Kim snickered.

"How are you going to explain to any man afterward how you came into your fortune?" Mya proposed disapprovingly.

"Girl, whatever. If they can't respect the hustle they can move around," Kim replied.

"I'll just Indecent Proposal somebody else," Amara said laughing.

Mya shook her head. She'd done all she could do and had to let her friend make her own decisions, disastrous as they seemed.

"Well you two hoes enjoy yourselves," Mya sighed, "I'm going back to bed. Amara?"

"What, girl."

"Be...careful."

7

Chapter 7

That night, sleep eluded Grayson like he was a kid waiting up for Santa Claus.

Not that he'd ever believed in Santa Claus, but still.

He'd definitely never had a childlike eagerness to sleep with someone before, but then again, never had sleeping with a woman been this premeditated for him.

There was still a chance that it may not happen, which was even more unique and he appreciated the distraction. It seemed that many firsts accompanied Amara, which was starting to give her a mystifying quality in his consciousness. This was going to be fun indeed, he thought. He didn't get far into that hedonistic anticipation before guilt began to overshadow it like a tropical storm.

He remembered that she was a virgin, and that he was, in this scenario, probably equivalent to the gross guy that tried to pick up girls during lunch by frequenting the high school he'd long since graduated.

Also, he realized that he liked Amara enough that perhaps he would've approached her eventually, without the money.

But this will protect them both, his head insisted, likely his second one. Amara had promised not to make this emotional, and though that seemed impossible knowing what he knew about her, he sensed she was smart enough to keep the consequences at bay and not bring them to his doorstep. He'd given her a whole night, and now would give her the entire day to rethink her decision. And yeah, the fact that they would spend the entire day together using his money in whatever way she wanted was probably not going to keep her in the most objective state but dammit, she was his guest. He wasn't a caveman.

When he arrived at the Palm Hotel the lobby's modern white decor was so pristine it was almost surreal. You would never know that there were impromptu performances and at least a baker's dozen entourage members smoking various plants and lounging around in it a few hours before.

He caught his reflection in the mirrored wall behind the concierge desk. At 34, he'd almost been an attractive male longer than he had not, but every once in awhile his reflection still startled him. He looked like every good-looking asshole jock in high school combined. He was now king of the asshole jocks.

He was dressed smartly in a navy sport coat with a crisp, blinding white polo underneath and khakis. He'd vacillated between showing up casual to put her at ease and trying to look his best for her and give her a weekend that would blow all of her future suitors out of the water. He felt he'd landed somewhere in the middle, but by the time he got to the desk he was greeting a distant old feeling of self doubt.

"Can you ring room 1703 and tell Amara Riley that Grayson Davis is waiting for her in the lobby, please," he told the concierge.

"Lucky girl," the concierge couldn't resist as she picked up the receiver. She was an attractive brunette with a British accent, which used to be his weakness.

Used to be?

"She's on her way down, sir. Anything else I can do for you?" Her professional demeanor returnined as though he'd imagined her comment. He returned her polite smile as he declined the offer.

Amara must've ran down, because not a moment later she was standing in front of him like the most delightful acid trip ever, in a bright yellow racerback jersey dress, fitted at her small waist and flared out past the knees. She should've looked like a giant banana but instead she was striking and regal, the brownness of her skin almost giving a severity to the whimsy of the dress. Dark skin, bright colors. He made a mental note. Her locs were down again and brushed almost completely to one side. There was a slight curl to them and they looked almost beachy. With her stylish sunglasses she did indeed look like she may've been famous, yet when she saw him her jaw dropped, and she playfully put the slender fingers of her right hand to the side of her mouth. She was quite girly, he was starting to notice. The feminine gesture brought a smile to his face.

"I'm underdressed yet again," she said to him quietly. He could've easily moved in for a kiss somewhere, anywhere on her face but he didn't. Patience is a virtue, he said to himself. One that he rarely had the need to exercise these days. He wasn't all that worried about her changing her mind, and now that he'd seen her looking like some kind of exotic dessert, he wasn't sure he would let her.

"Don't be silly, you look gorgeous, yet again." he assured her.

"Where are we going?" she purred excitedly.

Holy shit, she was hot. He'd been foolishly expecting a polite office version of Amara, or perhaps even the timid girl who showed up to a party not knowing what to expect. Not the flirty virgin, oozing sexuality, who now knew she was worth a million dollars— at least— and had more than likely been up most of the night as he had, thinking about the evening to come. Grayson instantly put his self doubt by the wayside and turned his settings to "full billionaire."

"Do you like seafood?" he asked as he offered her his arm. They walked through the lobby and out into the perfect California weather.

"Let's just say if I was stranded on a desert island, I would not put out an S.O.S.," she replied.

"Then I hope you haven't had breakfast because if so, you're going to hurt yourself at this place," he hyped.

"Red Lobster, I knew it!!" she said with sarcastic excitement, pumping a fist.

"You hit the jackpot today, girl," he said smoothly.

She laughed soundlessly, amused that he already felt comfortable enough with her to start ending his sentences with "girl." It was already the best day she'd ever had in her life and she had to keep forcing her mind to the present so she wouldn't overplay her charm hand and screw it all up.

That thing that seemed to happen wherever he went was now happening again, Amara noticed: a flurry of activity, people moving frantically as he moved, and then things simply appearing. It was as though the entire world around him was enchanted and she watched with fascination, though no one seemed to notice her, only him. He was always respectful and polite to all, saying "please" and "thank you" wherever necessary. But other than that, hardly any words were spoken and she was left to deduce what was happening after the fact.

On this occasion, as they walked down the entrance stairs someone directed them to stand to the side, a "please" and a "thank you" exchanged. Grayson continued to make small talk with her, and then was suddenly handed a set of keys. A beautiful black Mercedes convertible appeared before them with tan stitched leather, and they were directed to get in it. She wasn't even entirely sure he owned this car or not, but she had to assume he did.

The traffic was bumper to bumper so that they were basically still in front of the hotel. Amara sensed a strange energy, almost like she was being watched, but she shook it off. She turned in the passenger seat to face him, her body facing forward and her chin resting on her bare left shoulder.

"So, I'm dying to know what they said to you downstairs, last night after you left." Amara volunteered.

He huffed and smiled, his eyes on the road. "Basically... they asked what happened and I told them the truth."

"Which was?" she asked.

"That it was late and you were tired."

"No, *you* were tired," She shook her head, smiling. "And then they of course made fun of you."

"How did you know?" he sarcastically replied.

"Did you come back with anything?"

He laughed and glanced over at her before returning his eyes to the road. "Sort of."

"What did you say?" she wondered, already giggling in anticipation.

He smiled and took in a breath. "They basically said that I should've went for it anyway... to which I replied, 'not in a shithole like this,'" he regaled.

"Oh God, and they friggin' loved that," Amara growled, rolling her eyes behind her sunglasses.

"Right again," he laughed.

"Trash talking amongst men knows no color, I guess."

"Apparently not," he said. After a moment passed he continued. "Can I say something that could possibly be misconstrued as racist?"

"Please do, I've been waiting," she said.

"You've been waiting?"

"No, I mean like, ready to get it over with."

Grayson cocked his head to the side with a look and then pressed on. "You seem to be able to... maneuver rather seamlessly between worlds. Black and white, I mean. Does that make sense?"

She frowned, and he glanced towards her in time to see her furrowed brow and shaking head, as though ignorant of what he could be referring to.

Another joke. He smiled. Her expression softened. She let her gaze linger on him through her glasses while he looked straight ahead.

"I can't be the first person you've ever met like that," she said.

"No, not the first," he confirmed. "And different ethnicities, of course. You remind me of my friend Bel," he said.

"As in Bel Hafiz, the creator of MeTv," Amara confirmed in wonderment.

He nodded. "But I admire your... fluency. You take it a step further by trying to make everyone feel comfortable. You use humor."

He was using his professional persona she could see now. The traffic was starting to let up and he looked ridiculously debonnaire switching the exquisitely smooth gears of the car.

"I grew up in suburbia, so I guess on some level it's all I've known," she started. "I was born in a pretty small town in the midwest. One of those with one supermarket, one street light, that whole bit. I moved to Nashville when I was in high school and it was pretty suburban by anyone else's standards but for me, seeing more than one or two other black families was a bit of a shock. Never met anyone who grew up like me until I was an adult."

"So what I'm seeing is really the discomfort of not feeling truly part of either world?" he concluded.

Damn, he was hot when he did that.

Amara turned to look straight ahead. Her body had at some point twisted in his direction.

"My goodness. I didn't know a psychoanalysis was going to be part of the deal," she said.

"I need to know the fitness of your mental state," he bantered.

"Makes me wonder what else you've been deducing about me," she mumbled.

He unconsciously burst into a mischievous sideways grin as he glanced over at her. She was still staring at the road with a faint smile in her eyes.

He shifted from third to fourth gear on the highway and the wind whipped around them.

"You really want to know?" he teased. He had to raise his voice over the wind noise and the engine revved.

Amara bit her lip as her smile reached full wattage. Her volume matched his. "Not yet."

* * *

They finally made it to the restaurant that looked like a hole in the wall along the pier.

They sat at a table overlooking the water. Everything seemed to be made of driftwood and wide windows with no panes. It wasn't as high falutin' as Red Lobster, but it was one of his favorite places, and he knew Amara would love it.

As soon as they were seated the hostess asked, "Shall I have the waiter order The Works for you, Mr. Davis?" and Grayson politely confirmed.

They watched fishing boats roll in and out as they chatted and joked about various things. Amara told him about the elaborate journey of her packed belongings, and how they ended up in her hotel without ever having seen them once since Dale had picked her up.

"How'd you like first class?"

"It was business class actually, and it was a lovely 90 minutes," Amara answered.

"Cheap bastard," Grayson said.

"We can't all have private planes," she protested. "I thought it was more than generous of him. He was very accommodating."

Grayson was smiling but he suddenly, guardedly said, "I'm done talking about Dale."

Amara just stared at him. She couldn't tell if he was serious. She got the sense he was.

"He only spoke highly of you, if that's what you're worried about."

"I'm not worried about anything, I just don't want to talk about him," he said.

"Damn," she said, playfully disappointed. "Now I really, really want to talk about him."

"Well I don't," his blue eyes abruptly meeting her brown ones, penetrating them. He was either angry, or about to ravish her.

She looked at the water, fleeing his intense gaze. Part of her wanted to push him further, but she didn't dare.

"Okay... wanna talk about you then?"

"Not really," he frowned as he shook his head, tracing his fingers along the coaster under his glass.

Amara nearly offered herself up as a topic but she didn't want to risk his adverse reaction. Plus she didn't much feel like talking about herself either, not when her future was infinitely more interesting.

"What, then shall we discuss?" she wondered aloud.

"Your breasts," he said.

Her shoulders went concave with a soft chuckle.

"What about them?"

"Let me see them," he said lowering his voice.

"No," she blurted with a smirk.

Grayson squirted a slice of lemon in his mouth before adding it to his glass. "Please," he said.

Amara broke into laughter. She twirled the straw in her glass with a finger.

"Not really the best dress for that sort of thing," she continued shyly.

"If you were wearing a different dress, would you?"

"Would I what?" Amara said smiling, trying to get him to ask her again.

"Show me your boobs," he asked her again.

Amara cackled in a high pitch squeal as he simply stared at her, amusement in his eyes.

"It's comforting to know that underneath every successful genius billionaire is just... a dude," she conceded.

"As it is knowing under every erudite, young, exotic thing in a bright yellow dress is just a woman," he replied.

"There it is," Amara sighed, her eyes widening for a moment as she toyed with her water glass.

"What?"

"'Exotic.'"

"You don't like being exotic?" he asked.

"I'm not exotic."

"Isn't that subjective?" he argued.

"You're not exotic to me," she posited. "If I pass you every day, and one day you decide to notice me, I fail to see how that makes me exotic."

"Certainly there's more to familiarity than proximity, Amara. You think the reason men don't approach you is because they don't notice you?" he asked, a faint trace of disbelief in his voice. "Because I can tell you right now that's fucking ridiculous."

"My alma mater was 3 percent minority. Not black, I'm talking all minorities," Amara relayed. "You know what kind of dating pool specifically chooses a university to attend that's only 3 percent minority? Not the kind that's interested in Amara Riley, that's who."

"Irrelevant," he flatly said.

"Is that so," Amara laughed at his self assurance.

"I guarantee you it was a matter of intimidation, not lack of interest."

"Oh God, if one more person tells me I'm intimidating I'm going throw myself into that river, right there," Amara groaned.

"If I were your age, and not a billionaire, I'd be intimidated by you," Grayson said undeterred.

"Really?" Amara answered as if enlightened. "So if we were born at the same time, attended the same school, and were in the same classes, and talked like we're talking now, you wouldn't have asked me out?"

"Absolutely not."

"What?!" Amara shrieked.

Grayson explained, apologetic. "The Grayson you're describing is not the Grayson you know now, so no, I would not have been asking you out."

Amara seemed dismayed so he continued.

"For guys it's a simple matter of odds. If we don't think a girl would be into us, given the odds, we likely won't try. And even with a formula we strike out. A lot. It takes a toll on the psyche."

"When did you ever strike out?" Amara scoffed.

"Well....never. I mean, not really. But I never really tried until I was about your age."

"About the time you created Webster?" she inquired.

"Well, it wasn't called that, but yeah I suppose so," he recalled.

"So what changed?"

"I became... exotic," he raised his eyebrows as he said the word. He sipped his drink.

Amara smiled. "Yeah, I've seen the before pictures."

He laughed. "Have you seen Dale's?"

"I thought we weren't talking about him?" Amara teased.

"I'm always willing to talk about Dale's emo phase," Grayson replied enthusiastically.

"You know he almost picked up the wrong black girl at the airport?" Amara dished.

Grayson chuckled triumphantly as he looked towards the boats on the water, his profile turning Amara's mouth to a desert. "That fucking loser," he calmly smirked. Amara giggled.

* * *

Lunch went on lazily and deliciously. Each of them were charming yet guarded towards the other. Even when it became obvious in the silences that their minds were on other things, they never admitted it. He watched her watch the scenery, eating and savoring every morsel as though it were her last. Everything was the catch of the day. She marveled as fresh things were fished out with large nets, brought to the kitchen or sometimes directly to the table, and diversely prepared. After several courses of this she indeed nearly hurt herself.

"Oh my God," she sighed, sounding content yet concerned.

"Good?" he simply inquired.

"Yes. I don't get why you seem fine."

"I've already learned my lesson once," he said, taking a swig of a beer.

"I'd do it again," she said wincing.

He laughed and glanced at his watch.

Jesus, it was only 3pm. It was the longest day in history. He should've been savoring the infinite nature of the moment, the fact that he was genuinely enjoying her company, but on some level he couldn't. Couldn't stop thinking about tonight. He cursed the lengthy summer days.

He absently took another morsel of food to his mouth as he said, "If this is any indication of your overall appetite then I must tell you, I'm pretty excited."

The comment was meant to make her laugh but instead she seemed to grow anxious and was silent for a moment before she spoke with a confessional tone.

"So...I've put off telling you this for long enough..."

His stomach dropped to his ankles.

Dear God please no... she's not backing out of this is she? he thought.

He was silent as the grave as she continued.

"So, I told my friends about our... arrangement."

"Friends with an 's'?"

"Yes, two of my closest friends Mya and Kim. Mya's my roommate and Kim is a lawyer back in Nashville."

"Uh huh," he urged.

"So Kim was totally all for it—"

"And Mya?"

"...Pretty sure Mya hates you now, but back to Kim, who's the reason I bring this up."

"Okay."

"So....'member how I told you she was a lawyer?"

"Five seconds ago? Yes."

"Well... she... drew up a contract. For us. Well... for me."

Grayson was staring at her when he suddenly broke into a smile at her words, as if she was the cutest thing living. Amara involuntarily stopped breathing.

"Let me see it." he slowly blinked.

She reached into her bag and found her phone while he fished his out of his coat pocket. Her hands were trembling so she lowered the phone to her lap to keep them from view. When she did it gave him a few unobserved moments to drink her in, a single digit grazing back and forth across his lips as he did so.

She opened her Webster app and sent him the link, hearing the vibration of his own phone within seconds. Then it was her turn to watch him. She studied his eyes as he quickly, adeptly skimmed over the legalese, taking whole pages in within seconds, intermittently grinning from ear to ear.

At one point his eyes went wide and he glanced up at her. She knew which part he'd gotten to. Her hands flew to cover her face, meeting her head halfway down.

"A pull out clause?"

"She wrote it, not me," her voice muffled behind her hands.

"Tell your friend I really like her." he said dryly as he continued.

She peeked at him through her fingers as he got to the end.

"What are you thinking?" she asked.

"I'm thinking you're lucky to have a friend who's a lawyer."

"You're not offended?"

He chuckled. "I'm offended that you would think I would be offended."

Amara sat back and let a gust of air out of inflated cheeks.

Grayson snickered into his beer bottle, phone still in the other hand. "You were worried about that contract this whole time?" he grinned.

"Well pardon me if I'm not well versed in the art of sex negotiation," she defended sarcastically.

"A little louder for tables in the back."

"Sorry," she laughed. He glanced up at her from his phone as he got to the electronic signature page.

"Haven't heard one of those in awhile," he smirked. Amara returned his grin shyly.

Another tense silence followed that would soon become one of their last, because suddenly Grayson said:

"So technically, once I sign this, that means we can... start."

He looked at her then, with eyes completely unveiled and desire nakedly radiating through them.

Amara didn't know if she was nauseous, horny, scared, or near death. Her body seemed to be responding to his gaze as if it were so unfamiliar with the stimulation, it just started doing anything in response.

Grayson couldn't help snickering. He shook his head. His eyes glittered and he looked at her with admiration.

"You look positively terrified right now," he said.

"Because a second ago, my biggest problem was telling you about that contract and now..."

Grayson hit send and the phone warbled, sending an immediate confirmation. He set the phone down.

"And now you have a bigger problem," he finished as he took a drink from his beer bottle, his gaze on her.

Oh boy.

Amara's pulse quickened. There was no hope of calming her trembling body. She never felt so elated to be terrified.

Still, she couldn't resist. He walked right into it. On purpose, probably.

"How big?" she teased returning his gaze with a raised eyebrow, trying to even the score.

No chance of that.

Grayson just about murdered her with a single wink as he took a swig of his beer. He lowered the bottle, mouth still full of booze.

"Yeah right," she bluffed in a bout of nervousness, her tongue retreating to a corner of her mouth as she smiled.

"Now who's stereotyping who?" he said sitting back, pulling a wallet out of his breast pocket.

Her heart wouldn't stop doing flips, as though she had just reached the peak of a roller coaster.

Was this her life?? No, it wasn't, it was infinitely better than what she could have envisioned on her own.

Had she really captured his imagination the way he'd captured hers? It just didn't seem possible. She felt a bit panicky. She had a feeling she would be trying to catch her breath for the rest of the night. She suddenly felt grossly out of shape.

As if he'd read her mind, he continued.

"If it makes you feel any better, you terrified me first. Because for a moment I thought you were going to tell me that you were backing out of the deal."

Her voice was barely audible.

"You were terrified?"

"Yes."

Grayson looked Amara over. Her nipples were pronouncing themselves through her bra, enough that he could see them through her dress.

He continued.

"I was terrified because what started out as an innocent attraction to you has become..." he took a moment to search for the right words, "an unignorable fixation."

His words infused her with equal parts fear, curiosity and confidence. She was glad he'd waited until now to make such a bewildering confession.

"How many of those have you had?" Amara deflected, nodding towards his beer.

Grayson didn't argue about defense mechanisms just then, he merely smiled, lifted his phone from the table and held it in front of his face. "Say cheese."

Then, the electronic simulation of a camera shutter.

"What was that for?" she asked.

"I'm calling it, 'the before picture.'" he said.

"Take one of yourself too," she said, sending him a flirting glance before looking down and fiddling with her napkin.

Grayson stared at her. Part of him thought maybe he should take her advice, but he didn't. He stared at her for a long time. Even though he knew she could feel it, she didn't look up.

He looked at her lips, barely believing that the wait was suddenly about to be over.

She shifted her posture as their waiter came to clear the table, as if she was bored.

"Anything else I can get for you guys?" the waiter dutifully asked.

Grayson kept his gaze on Amara. "Just the check."

8

Chapter 8

K issing Amara once they got back into the car, Grayson realized a bit too late, had been his first mistake.

He hadn't meant anything by it other than to put her at ease.

He could tell she was nervous by the far-off look she'd adopted once he'd seen the contract and sent it back to her lawyer friend with his signature.

She'd obviously retreated to her head and, once there, likely put undue pressure on herself, obsessing over her body or some such detail.

So he figured if he could catch her off guard with a kiss, he could save her the awkwardness, and the hardest part would be over.

Instead, Amara's kiss had been like a match on a dry forest.

It was a gesture he'd used a million and one times: lean in, one hand to graze the cheek, hand moves to the mouth, one kiss on the lips. He wouldn't call it a signature move, but it was his custom when selecting a woman for his next affair. He liked when a car ride was fraught with all kinds of anticipation; he found a fast ride in a luxury car could sometimes do the job better than foreplay or was sometimes foreplay in itself.

Not so with Amara.

Because when he leaned in, her eyes locked onto his and willed them to remain open and return her gaze.

And when he touched her, ever so slightly, she sucked in a breath so sharp and yet her eyes barely fluttered— a reaction so foreign and unexpected it positively electrocuted him.

When his hand moved to her mouth, she had yielded so utterly and completely, it was as though he had known her before, but he hadn't and it had only made him more anxious to make that happen.

Finally the kiss came, and it was hungrier that he would've liked, her eyes still wide open and watching his, moving back and forth between him and their connecting lips, which didn't take long to be their connecting tongues, and then back to their mouths, the sound of their panting and their smacking lips, so good, so tantalizingly slow, and he completely forgot where they were and what they were supposed to be doing, and the top was still down and anyone who was anyone could see them.

When they finally came up for air, all Grayson could say was, "Wow."

Amara finally closed her eyes once he pulled away, full lips parted and a pained expression on her face as if searching for his kiss. Her eyes darted underneath her eyelids a bit before they fluttered open to the sound of the car engine revving up.

Oh, right, she thought. *Car. Planet Earth. My name is Amara.* The car took off like a rocket down the street.

"I gotta get you home. Now," Grayson said.

"Where's home?" Amara asked dreamily.

"Not close enough," he said.

He stole kisses between every traffic light, bringing her tortuously higher and higher to boiling point until she didn't seem to be able to come down anymore.

The car stalled at one particularly lengthy stop, and he swore as he struggled to regain his mental coordination, his fellow drivers honking horns and yelling out appreciative sentiments. Normally Amara would be laughing, telling some joke to put him at ease, but she was in no state to be of use, and it was good to see that they both seemed to be suffering under the same spell.

At one point he freed his right hand in order to trail it up her dress at the knee, and when he discovered she had been so wet that it was starting to pool between her lower thighs he almost ran off the road and killed them both. How had he not remembered to put the top up before now? He was starting to try and convince himself that losing your virginity on the side of the road in a car could be special too.

"You have protection, right?" Amara broke through his thoughts.

"No way, I love paternity suits," he answered sharply, sarcastically.

Amara was silent but not because of his response. She was staring at his erection that had become bold and triumphant beneath his khakis. When she reached out to touch it, he forcefully put her hand back in her lap, which then caused his hand to roguely yet gently continue its pilgrimage back to the wetness between her thighs. This time, Amara parted her legs for him and he let out a groan and cursed.

While she watched his eyes, conflicted between the road and the discovery of his own hand, the hand was starting to fondle her.

"How much farther?" Amara demanded.

"Almost there," he said.

"Me too," she laughed in a thin voice.

Grayson retracted his wayward hand, now wet with Amara's juices. Two of his fingers went into his mouth as if he'd asked to lick the bowl from the batter of a cake. The car slowed and they took a right turn down a street that was practically straight up the side of a mountain.

"I'm feeling really weird right now," Amara suddenly announced.

"What do you mean?" he managed to ask.

"I mean I don't have any feeling left in my hands and I need water. I think I'm having an allergic reaction to something."

"I think you're describing arousal," he smiled.

"No, I know what arousal feels like, this feels like I'm about to die."

"Have you been this aroused before? Because I haven't. Not from foreplay," he confessed.

"When does it go away," she said between coughs.

"You don't want it to." he giggled. "At least I don't."

"We're gonna die on this hill first," she said.

Amara felt as if she were completely vertical as they wound up the endless hillside. As a breathtaking view emerged on the driver side, the road finally evened out and they were in front of a large private estate. They abruptly stopped. As she took in the house that spanned her entire field of vision, Grayson was out of the car and on the passenger side in a flash, wrenching Amara from the car and standing her up against the passenger side door. His mouth plundered hers without ceremony and her arms went up around his neck, into his closely shorn hair, and then down along his shoulders. They could've had sex right there but she figured that if he'd risked their lives to get here that he'd probably wait until they got inside—

Suddenly the rogue hand had returned under her dress.

His fingers had found the oasis between her thighs and began to separate the fabric of underwear. With expert precision, they found her clitoris and began to rub steadily. Her mouth flew open as she tensed, her eyes shut tight as she held onto his broad shoulders, paralyzed as pleasure was coursing through her, building at a furious rate. His breathless kisses up and down her neck and along her jawline were sweet enough to make her cry, the contrast between the tenderness of his lips and the wicked machinations of his fingers making her whisper velvety curses into his neck.

With his own throaty encouragements tickling her ear between licks and kisses it wasn't long before she felt release rising up to meet her. Fuckin' a, it felt so good already, and the feeling was only getting stronger. Her orgasm was going to be a supernova.

"Wanna watch me come?" she heard someone say, someone that sounded *exactly* like her. Gruffly he assured her he did, again and again. As she bucked and gasped uncontrollably against him and his Mercedes, her orgasm radiating through her ferociously, he continued to rub and lick and suck her all the way back down to the present.

"Holy shit, Amara. You. Are. Incredibly. Sexy," he whispered as he straightened her underwear, then her dress. "I almost lost it just watching that."

He kissed her lightly as he pulled away from her and took her hand. She looked around and realized they were still outside.

She hated that she even had legs as he started to pull her, hated that they weren't lying down. The friction of her thighs and underwear against her still swollen sex caused aftershocks in her as she walked.

Amara tried to remember a time where she'd seen a more luxurious house in person and not just in pages of a magazine. High ceilings, modern and mostly gleaming white, mixed with complements of dark wood that felt both masculine and old world. It was a statement of elegance by way of arrogance, from a man who did not grow up having money and was determined to show he had better plans for it than anyone. She was certain she'd never seen greener grass. The panoramic views were to die for, but she had the feeling those would have to wait.

He'd retrieved his phone with a free hand, hauling Amara behind with the other. He appeared to be taking a phone call but instead, whatever he was doing had brought the entire house to life. Suddenly the doors unlocked and they were inside.

Soft light emitted from mysterious sources embedded in the decor, the level of detail reserved for the very wealthy and selective. Even the silence that welcomed them seemed to be of a quality that was beyond her means. Her size ten strappy platforms sank into the luxurious carpet, that turned to luxurious tile, and finally to luxurious hardwood.

"I hate the size of this house right now," he said, trapping her in the hallway outside of a random guest bedroom. Amara laughed as he kissed her this way and that, her wits having returned to her now that he'd brought her to orgasm once, in the driveway against the side of his convertible.

"I need to... calm down," he suddenly said.

"Why?" she replied, sounding disappointed.

His head was laying on one of her shoulders, his hands moving up and down her naked arms. She could feel his hot panting breath on her neck as he found his words again.

"It's your first time, Amara I can't..." he gave her shoulders a squeeze as his voice trailed off.

The weight of him against her felt sweet. She put a hand in his hair and took in her surroundings as she reluctantly reminded him, "It's your million."

Fuck. He was paying her for this, he remembered.

The sickness of the thought gave him the motivation he needed to get his bearings.

He kissed her sweetly- not on those lips- before retreating down the hallway and into the guest bedroom where he discarded his sports coat and walked out of sight around a corner.

When she followed him she was greeted by a sun-soaked balcony and deckchairs.

Grayson had walked behind a wet bar that was catty-corner to an outdoor sitting area that overlooked the mountains above and the city below. Amara kicked off her shoes and sauntered towards him.

"Drink?" he offered.

"No thanks," Amara replied.

He smiled. "Non-alcoholic if you prefer."

"Bad manners to turn down a drink, is it?" she bantered, knowing he must think her a prude.

"Not bad manners, just bad etiquette. A subtle difference."

"Fine. An Alaskan polar bear heater." she countered.

He laughed. It was a reference from the original Nutty Professor movie, 1963.

"'You gonna drink this or rub it on your chest?'" he recited.

"Orange peel, lemon peel, carrot!!" she giggled.

He could still smell her on his fingers as he raised the glass to his lips.

"If I'm a little young for the reference, then you definitely are."

"My dad grew up going to the movies and sitting in front of the tv," she explained. "He's seen just about any and everything that's ever been filmed."

"Sounds like an interesting guy," he replied.

Amara's mind went to her father, her mother's abuser.

For some reason, she had never had trouble separating the man from his abuse.

It was hell when he was there, but once he'd agreed to leave, their relationship had instantly improved. She was thirteen then. And now, they were cool and shared a Netflix account. She was just paranoid that one day she would wind up marrying him and living her mother's life all over again.

But she didn't say any of that.

"He's a basket case," was all she said, as she grabbed the drink from his hand and took a sip. It was strong, whatever it was. She grimaced as it went down.

"Ready?" she sputtered.

Grayson smirked. He kept his eyes on her as he moved from behind the bar with purpose and walked her backward by both hands. They passed the sitting area, located directly in front of large folding glass panels that served as the guest bedroom walls.

"How do you take this infernal dress off?" he asked, giving her a once over.

"I have to pull it up over my head," she smiled.

"Do it," he said.

"Out here?" she shyly asked.

She never wanted to seem too eager, he realized, as though not quite knowing what she was allowed and never wanting to overstep her bounds.

It was the reason why she'd made a monetary deal for herself rather than simply say, "do you want to be my boyfriend?"

He knew that was what she wanted, knew that he couldn't give it to her, so he had let her make the arrangement.

The more he tasted of her, the more his decision made a crater in his guts.

She was pure marriage material, a former employee, and now he was using her for sex. He was low indeed for this.

But he pushed his thought process aside as she stood in front of him, tossing her sunglasses on the table behind her and lifting her skirt up above her hips with long dark limbs. She pulled her dress over her head and her matching bra and panties were lacy, and also yellow. His libido put his conscience into a sleeper hold.

"You borrow those too?" he asked.

"No," she smiled. "These I've been saving for a special occasion."

Shit.

No choice but to make it special then, Davis, he thought to himself.

He left the wide balcony doors open behind them, making sure there was a bed within arm's reach before he kissed her again.

He cupped her face in his hands, her breath coming out in light gusts and this time, her eyes were closed. The afterglow of her previous orgasm by now had faded. She was ready again, and the same intensity he'd felt between them in the convertible was back.

After a long moment, he still hadn't kissed her, and those dark eyes of hers flew open and found his impossibly blue ones like a tractor beam. The two seemed to instinctively know that their kiss was going to transport them again, and they each would be lost. He touched his forehead to hers and she let out a sigh as she smiled, he did the same.

Holy shit, this is crazy, she wanted to say. But she didn't move, because now his head was tilted and he was leaning in, their lips brushing at first and then clasping, one tender kiss after another. She tried to stay calm, tried to let him take his time, but she was holding her breath and it was backing up into her lungs.

She was indeed coming apart in his arms, just as he'd predicted she would.

"Breathe, Amara," he simply said.

Like he'd said to her when he was still her boss and he'd ambushed her in the Webster cafeteria, and she wanted to cry again like she did then.

"*Fuck*, it's happening again," she sobbed. She broke away from him and looked down at her hands, palms up, flexing open and closed at her command. "I can't feel them," she was panicking.

"Just relax, Amara," he grabbed both her wrists and forced her eyes to meet his. There were tears in them and her breathing remained fractured. He couldn't fault her, because it was just as intense for him, only he had had lots and lots of sex.

"Do you want to stop?" he dared to ask, his raging erection protesting in horror.

"No it's just... God, it's just too much," she panted. He laughed breathlessly. "How are people having sex like this?"

"It's not like this with everyone," he explained.

"Just don't kiss me," she said, starting to calm down.

"Okay," he agreed, grinning.

"Because it's just... I don't know, it's too good..." she admitted.

"Too good?" he confirmed, with arrogance in his gentle voice.

She nodded her head innocently as he left the closeness of her warmth to try and even the score on nakedness. He crossed his arms at his sides and discarded his shirt, revealing his bare chest which was mostly devoid of any hair. He was pleasantly defined but not chiseled, as though he used to work out furiously but had stopped. His large hands locked onto her hips and pulled her close. Her arms shot up and around his shoulders as his hands perused her body. Now they were skin to skin and she enveloped all his senses, making him feel dizzy.

Damn. She was incredibly soft and he leaned in to kiss her again, but barely nipped her bottom lip as she pulled away.

"No kissing," she teased.

"Shit, I forgot," he said, making her giggle. "Lay down."

Amara reluctantly left his embrace and walked around him towards the bed, hoping he was watching her from behind as she laid down.

He was.

He dropped his trousers unashamedly, his substantial erection protruding through his black boxer briefs.

Amara shrieked a little and drew her hands up to her face.

She felt the weight of his body sink onto the bed, hover over her form and settle down next to her. Next, she felt his hands on her belly and she tensed. He leaned into her ear.

"You can keep your eyes covered for this next part if you want." he conceded, with a kiss on her cheek.

She felt his body shift over her again. She started to guess what was next as she felt his hands on her lacy underwear, pulling them down.

Here we go, she thought.

She sensed him stretching his long torso across her and heard a lot of fiddling, a drawer, the sound of a wrapper.

"What are you doing?" she wondered. She could've just dropped her hands but now she was committed.

"Shush," he told her, intent on the task of easing a condom onto his throbbing erection. He looked up at Amara's covered face to see if she was looking but judging from her energy she genuinely didn't seem to be peeking. A smile drew up one corner of his mouth.

"Ready?" he said.

"Yeah," she replied, almost like a question, sounding decidedly un-ready.

His weight shifted indiscriminately yet again. She suddenly felt the heat of his large firm hands parting her thighs wide. She willed herself out of a panic, her body trembling. Then, an appreciative growl as he cursed softly.

She'd never heard him do that, she thought, as she involuntarily licked her lips. She let out a light gasp as he abruptly grabbed her by the hips and dragged her forward on the bed several inches.

Suddenly she felt... heat? Wetness? Holy shit was that his tongue on her—

Her arms flew to her sides as she used them to sit up and look.

When she did, her eyes glanced down to see Grayson, fucking, Davis, fulfilling one of her favorite workday-wasting fantasies. Her jaw dropped as she stared at his head, the top half deliciously serene, the bottom concealed from her vision by *her own naked body.*

She laid back down instantly in disbelief.

"Oh my God," she whispered.

She put the back of her hand to her mouth, her eyes going to and fro at the sensation.

"Oh my God," she said again, louder this time.

The tip of his tongue zeroed in on the nub at her center and rapidly stimulated it for a long moment before he was back to sucking and licking and teasing.

She grabbed a pillow and put it over her face and shouted into it, "OH MY GOD."

"Good?" he briefly asked, coming up for air.

She removed the pillow and let out an appreciative dirty sentiment. Then another.

"I'm gonna marry your fucking tongue," she moaned.

The thin, frail tone of her voice was sending torrents of pleasure coursing through him. She continued torturing him with more choice words until he was eating like mad and digging his narrow fingers into her supple brown skin. He wanted to make her come but he was holding on by a thread. He pulled away from her and she gasped, partly from the loss of his kiss on her sex and partly because now he was kneeling over her, wildly naked and erect, his length shrouded in rubber.

He wiped his mouth and said, "Sorry babe, but I gotta be inside you or else I'll lose my mind."

Babe? Inside?

Amara laid back and let him situate her as if she were at a doctor's appointment. He was hoisted on his sturdy arms, rather high above her she thought, and she didn't know whether to look up at him or *down* at him.

Up, she decided.

She was as ready as a virgin could possibly get. His erection nudged impatiently at the center of her. One of his arms disappeared to steady himself as he entered, reappearing at his side. So far, so good. She started to feel pressure more than pain, and what seemed like an internal wall blocking him. A tender groan escaped from his throat. Amara's heart skipped a beat and she studied his face, too timid to look fully into his eyes anymore.

"You okay?" he hastily asked.

She nodded. His weight shifted to his elbows and he came down to kiss her. He was only half paying attention she could tell, as she watched his eyes close and his expression morph, distantly aware of the taste of herself on his lips and chin.

"You feel so good already," he coaxed into her ear. Her bra was still on and he loosened the front clasp without difficulty, running a pale hand across her chest and taking one soft mound into his hand and onto his mouth. She sucked in a breath and he moaned his approval as though he knew her thoughts. The sight of his tongue stretching out to tease her dark areola sent a rushing ache to her pelvis, and like magic he started to sink further inside.

"That's it," he groaned, "let me in."

At that, another fierce tingling enveloped her middle and she felt her body accepting the rest of him, slowly at first and then with force.

Involuntarily her eyes shut tight and her lips went into a pucker as she let out a faint sigh. Grayson let out a furious moan that seemed to surprise him.

He lay still for a while as if apprehensive to do anything. He began to sway and move and then gave her a modest thrust.

They both let out a curse at the same time.

They were now suddenly, savagely, connected. Amara's hands frantically traced his whole body as if he were a new appendage, while Grayson kept shocking her with intermittent thrusts, typically followed by a curse.

He breathed in and out, he shifted his weight. Amara was ridiculously lush, tight and wet. He was now one thrust away from completely losing it. He had painted himself into a pleasure corner and didn't know how to get out without embarrassing himself.

Amara instinctively started to lift her open leg. Grayson suddenly went rigid. "Nonononononononono. No," he exclaimed. Sounding strained.

Amara had to laugh.

"Tell me what I can do to help you right now," she chuckled.

His head was down so she could only hear him.

"Just keep laughing at me," he panted.

She did. Heartily and from her belly. When she did, she shed the last of her apprehension and she looked in his eyes as he raised his head, a faint look of... something in them. Amusement? Adoration? They were calm and alluring.

"You're beautiful," he said.

"*You're* beautiful," she insisted.

The thrusts were back again. She put one hand on his face as she looked into his eyes, but soon had to abandon the task as waves of pleasure demanded her attention. She threw her head back.

Amara was intoxicated. Every thrust felt like a second spent in heaven, and she wasn't shy about what he was doing to her. Her gaze came back to meet his. Her brow furrowed and her eyes went dark. She noticed he was watching her and her mouth went slack, tiny "yeah"s building up in her throat.

His short gusts of air hit her eyelids and the intermittent sounds of his aching pleasure sent her into raptures. He was in ecstasy, there was simply no other interpretation. The more she thought about what she was doing to him the more power she felt. And the more power she felt the more aggressive she became.

"Just like that," she said. It came out in a whisper.

But he'd heard it.

He let out a satisfied groan as his pace quickened and his thrusts became more insistent. Heaven began to stretch out longer and longer until the feeling was so potent and steady she could've sworn she was there.

"Grayson," she pleaded.

"What, baby," he panted, relentless pleasure turning him into a kitten.

"I think I'm gonna c—"

Amara exploded.

All she could see was the inside of her eyelids as an intense release of bliss washed over her. She couldn't breathe or speak or even hear, and the pleasure continued to thrash her as if she were being mauled by it. Distantly she could observe Grayson's own orgasm furiously tearing through him, seizing his body, making it nearly impossible for her to come down. The moment was ridiculously intimate, like two shell-shocked soldiers surviving an attack from a foxhole.

Finally, Grayson collapsed on top of her, slick with perspiration. When she finally found her voice she was overwhelmed with emotion.

"What the fuck was that?" she sobbed hoarsely.

Grayson, his face burrowed in Amara's smooth neck, managed to lift his lips to her ear.

"Round one," he simply said.

Without looking he raised a free hand until he could feel her face. He stroked the coarse strands of her hair until she was calm. With heavy eyelids, she turned her head towards his fingertips and kissed. Sleep had been the last thing on their minds since they'd first laid eyes on each other, and now that they were one it was the only thing they wanted. Their tranquility was immense, and it wasn't long before a dreamless sleep had overtaken them both.

9

Chapter 9

Amara woke lazily, her mind willing itself to alertness in the pitch dark guest bedroom. The patio doors were still open, and though the scene was beautiful against the outdoor lights, there was something a bit creepy about it. As though she were expecting a jungle predator to come around the corner, having wandered in through the patio doors. She looked around for a clock.

11:45 pm.

Oh man, she slept the entire day away. She sat up, feeling slicked and sore in unusual places.

Amara....

You. Just. Had. Sex, her head reminded her.

"And it was... damn good," she said aloud to herself.

She snickered, smushing her face into her pillow at the collection of new memories gathering. She emptied a scream into it that barely escaped. She felt other-worldly. The girls would never believe—

Her phone. She'd lost track of it. Was it still in the car?

The car. More flashbacks of the day shot through her. Sensation began to build in her groin instantly.

That's it, let me in, he'd said.

Oh, my God.

Her head retreated back into the pillow.

Where was that sexy bastard anyway? She thought with a wicked smile. She got up and sauntered toward the opulent bathroom, gave herself a long look in the mirror before starting the water and shutting the door.

* * *

Grayson, on the other hand, had been up for hours.

When he awoke, the daylight had turned dark blue and night was close on its heels. He must've slept like a dead man because he was still laying on top of the poor girl and he hadn't even gotten up to dispose of the condom, which never happens.

As he got up and entered the shower, he reflected on his million dollar indulgence with an unconscious grin. Worth every fucking penny and he still had four weeks to go. He noticed he felt full in a strange way he couldn't pinpoint. Perhaps he did only need one night with Amara.

But then the sex started to replay in his head, and his erection was immediately aggressive in protest.

Amara was a natural. Her body was sin. She was a dizzying variety of sweet and innocent one moment and boldly daring and dirty the next.

It won't be as good the next time, he cynically assured himself. They had unique chemistry, that's true. But it'd also been a while for him, and the first time for her. It was the best he'd had in recent memory, but that could be a fluke. So convinced he was of his theory that he was willing to do it again, just to prove it right.

By the time his shower was over it was indeed evening. Amara was a shapely shadow amid the stark white of his sheets. Her locs splayed across the pillows and one long arm was above her head so that she looked like a character in a hieroglyph. Suddenly he wanted to rouse her from sleep in all kinds of wicked ways. So much for that "one and done" nonsense. Right then his mind registered the insistent vibration of his phone. Were those texts he was getting?

What the hell was going on?

Grayson found it in the pocket of his discarded blazer.

52 notifications??

He saw three texts from Dale. A lot for him.

Hey, bud. Some amateur footage floating around of u and A going to 3rd base in the convertible. Gr8 wknd!!!

Okay. So, Dale was pissed.

Wasn't it his bright idea to bring Amara to the party? No culpability there.

Another right after it followed.

Tell A no need to return on Mon in case paps are sniffing around here. No one knows her ID.

He forgot Amara was still intent on fulfilling her notice. So dutiful. He snickered as he wondered how the third floor would manage without her.

The third was one word. All caps.

YET.

Next, he spotted an email from his publicist. Along with a pretty racy attachment.

"Care to comment?" was all it said.

"No." he simply answered back.

Well, shit.

He'd seen a few paps outside the hotel... but they'd been followed? He was used to a certain level of scrutiny, but this seemed a little more aggressive than usual.

Then again, he wasn't usually making out in broad daylight. He smiled as he reprimanded himself.

Oh well. The limits on his personal life were still what they'd always been. It would all blow over by the time the affair was over, he predicted.

He went to the kitchen and rummaged through his gargantuan refrigerator and found leftover Korean.

Score.

He fired up all six restaurant grade burners before stretching his long limbs at the dining room table and opening his laptop. Two bowls and three hours later, he was rewarded with Amara's presence in the dining room.

"Whatever that is smells amazing," she said huskily.

Her sudden appearance gave his heart a pleasant start, and he smiled.

"Well if it isn't sleeping beauty herself," he said.

She smiled and circled the table picking through various dishes before discovering which one held the rice. She grabbed a bowl and started to build, opting for the chopsticks instead of a fork. Her hair looked elegant sitting in a completely vertical bun on top of her head, a few long strands framing her face in the front. She was wearing one of his cashmere robes, a t-shirt and... were those his boxers? He scoffed.

"What," she lazily asked.

"You're adorable," he laughed, tenderness in his voice.

Laying it on thick, Davis? He thought to himself.

Amara beamed and bit her lip, and he was instantly ready for round two. She shook her head and looked up at the ceiling.

"Did we...?"

"We did," he said, failing to stifle a grin.

"Daaamn," she said with innocent eyes, looking out the panoramic windows at nothing but pitch darkness, and possibly her own reflection.

"How do you feel?" he said.

"Honestly?"

"Of course," he smiled. It's what he'd said to her that day in the conference room when she'd asked the same thing. Did she remember?

She looked over at him, quiet.

"I feel like I'm in love," she simply said.

Silence. The tension rose, but still, he returned her gaze.

"Not with you, with sex," she said. "What, did you think I meant you?" she asked confused.

"Ha ha," he dryly replied.

"You should've seen your face," she smiled, topping her bowl off.

"One prank and now you're a master," he said.

"All my things are still at the hotel, and I think I'm still checked in until tomorrow..." she started.

"I can have them brought here," he suggested.

She carried her bowl to the window sill across from him and sat against it, rather than next to him. He gazed at her statuesque legs.

"My flight leaves tomorrow evening, but I was thinking maybe I could cancel it and... we could drive?"

"Yeah... about that," he began.

Her heart jolted sickly.

No way he was done already. She wasn't, not by a longshot. Jeez, did everyone except her tire of things so easily? She expected that from just about anyone but him.

"Or I can keep my flight," she appeased. "And, I don't know, maybe after work, I could—"

"You're not going back to work," he cut her off.

A jolt of a different kind went through her, and she wondered if she could die from all the adrenaline.

"But I still have a week to go," she weakly protested.

"Have you looked at any media devices since you've been awake?"

"No, and I think I left my phone in the front seat of your convertible, along with my dignity," she shot back.

They exchanged a knowing look that bloomed into a smile.

"We were followed," he informed her.

Amara didn't quite understand because she was a regular person.

"By... the cops?"

"By the paparazzi," he chuckled.

"Oh my gosh!" she guffawed. "When? Outside the hotel? I knew I felt like people were watching me."

He turned his laptop toward her, and she was confronted with grainy shots from various angles of a black girl in a fancy convertible, writhing around like a slut with no shame, wearing a yellow dress and looking conspicuously like her.

Amara put down her bowl and leaned in with shock. She was mortified. It had felt poetic at the moment, while it was happening to her, but now she was watching it, and she looked like some kind of zoo animal trying to give birth. And now it was being plastered everywhere, probably replayed by randos, and everyone that had ever known her. Her parents, her co-workers, her college professors, people she went to church with. That old guy at the grocery store that always pulled a basket out for her when he saw her. She was pretty sure that guy had an internet connection.

Amara sat on the edge of the window sill, her head in her hands.

"So far it's just pictures, no story. It's still early, and no one knows who you are. Yet," he echoed Dale's words.

"And if I go into work then they'll figure it out," she deduced, her voice still muffled by her hands.

"Dale doesn't want headquarters to become a circus."

"Oh my God, Dale has seen these..." she panicked.

Dale?

"Yeah, Dale saw them. What does that matter?" he asked.

She dropped her hands from her face.

"It matters to me that he thinks I'm a slut and that he's seen my 'oh' face, that's hella awkward," she countered.

"Well seeing as how you'll probably never see Dale again, and he doesn't consider you a friend in any capacity, I think you're safe."

Amara tried not to seem offended by the outburst, but then again she didn't see how she couldn't be.

She was going to make light of it but found she didn't want to.

She looked at him. He had apology in his eyes but said nothing more about it.

He sighed. "We might be holed up here for awhile, in case this thing doesn't blow over. I have a few events I have to attend, some of which can't be canceled. Then I have a summit in Montenegro in three weeks or so. It'll be a few days, but it might be wise for you to stay here. You're a homebody, aren't you Amara?"

"Was it that obvious?" she said, echoing their beach conversation.

"Only if you're paying attention," he grinned.

The guy had a memory on him. She smiled, the gesture putting her at ease with him.

"I have no clothes," she lamented.

He shrugged. She gave him a wicked glare, and he smiled again.

"That can easily be remedied," he finally said.

"How? Online?"

"The store can come to us."

"Ooooh!" her eyes were wide and childlike. "And the food too?" she added excitedly.

"Well yes, but I think that's just called 'delivery.'"

"Oh, right," she remembered. She suddenly sighed.

"You mean there really won't be jetsetting of any kind?"

Grayson smiled. "Had your heart set on it, did you?"

"It's just that it's so, like my life, that the one time I land a billionaire, he can't take me anywhere."

"Come here," he said.

If his voice turned her on before, sex with him had sent it to another level like a guitar amp. She reluctantly complied as if he were bothering her, and resigned herself to his lap.

"If the coast is clear in a couple of weeks, I'll take you wherever you want to go. Deal?"

He was wearing linen trousers and no shirt, and he smelled earthy and rich, like sexy oatmeal.

"I think... it's better just not to get my hopes up," she said faintly, her eyes becoming drowsy. Grayson's hands had begun roaming inside the cashmere robe, and she craned her neck to one side to accommodate his kisses that were slowly becoming more provocative.

"Speaking of getting things up," he flirted.

"I haven't finished my bowl," she said.

He released Amara from his clutches, and she grabbed her bowl from the edge of the table, returning to her place at the window sill. He sat facing her, and his erection was unabashed, as was her gaze on it as she chewed.

"That thing right there?" she began between bites, pointing her chopsticks at his groin, "my new favorite thing."

"You mean this old thing?" he pointed to his own erection and Amara nodded. Then he stood up and shed his trousers so that he was completely naked. He watched her drink him in, this time with hunger rather than nervousness. His cock jerked in response. Her eyes didn't stray as he walked towards her and grabbed her hand.

"Finished yet?" he inquired.

"What are you doing?" she smirked, setting her food down.

"You haven't seen the rest of the house," he said, stripping her of her robe. Her nipples protruded through his worn vintage t-shirt. He lifted it over her head, and his mouth went dry at the brazen sight of her slightly larger-than-perfect breasts. Her locs collapsed out of the bun they were in and tumbled down her shoulders.

"So rude, my mother would be horrified," he teased. The boxers were cute. He left them on and grabbed her hand as he led her on a tour of the estate, which ended at an unassuming door in the hallway. Behind the door, he revealed a descending staircase that led to his master bedroom.

"Are we meeting Colonel Mustard in the conservatory?" Amara asked, adopting an English accent.

"*Fuck*, you didn't tell me you did accents," he growled. Amara giggled.

Grayson had been wrong; it was better the second time.

Now that they knew what to expect they gave themselves over to it freely.

Amara was again a mixed bag of shy and aggressive, innocent and uninhibited. When she got on top, she kept trying to cover or close her eyes.

"Can we turn the lights out?" she asked.

"No," he muttered.

"What if I get so into it, that I slobber on you?"

"Welcome to my world," he said. She laughed. He smiled.

Grayson went to work, learning Amara's body. She was sensitive, but by no means fragile. Green, but completely confident in her body. He discovered that she liked being teased, which he wouldn't have guessed. She seemed enthusiastic to try oral sex, and though it wasn't really his thing, he let her. With very little learning curve she more than got the hang of it. His specialty however was making her come, which was his favorite, and also very very easy.

They had sex again and again until they were spent, until the blue light of day was back, only this time it was dawn. They were technically in the basement, yet his bedroom had floor to ceiling frameless windows with a view. While the top level faced the westernmost part of the city below, this one faced the eastern forest trees on the opposite side, part property line and part privacy fence. It was so beautiful that Amara came and stood in front of it and wept, as came to be her custom every morning when she woke up in Grayson's bed, his smart house setting her alarm at dawn each day. The first time she'd done it he crept up behind her and felt his way around her body like a blind man as he asked into her shoulder, "Are you okay?"

"No. Yes. It's very beautiful," she summarized, eyes and lips swollen with emotion.

"It is," he whispered, his gaze feasting on the aesthetic, her blue-black silhouette underneath his white hands. The contrast was a visual buffet that evoked a wildness in him every opportunity that he'd had to relish it. It made him question what he knew about life, about history. That every pale-skinned explorer he'd ever read, who found themselves in a far away land, seemed to leave out such a conspicuous discovery as the dark-skinned woman suddenly spoke volumes, far more intriguing than what they included— old letters droning on about flora and fauna and... gold.

Right. Like they'd never seen gold before.

Now here was Grayson, having joined the same secret society. The kind that spouted ideals and then littered the planet with golden infants that could be from anywhere and nowhere. It was his last conscious thought before he drifted to sleep, the sun creeping up the horizon.

10

Chapter 10

L ater that day, the morning after the pictures were released, the first headline was created.

"Grayson Davis Hot and Heavy In Public."

A handful of search engine-friendly nouns. Well played. And who wouldn't stop to read with a headline like that?

"Grayson Davis' Life is Better Than Yours."

That one was Amara's favorite.

Dale sent another text Tuesday afternoon: *A's now a TT on Webster, no name yet.*

TT as in trending topic.

Okay. So maybe this thing wasn't blowing over so easily.

"Dale says you're a trending topic on Webster," he parroted aloud from the couch in one of the living areas.

"I can't believe no one from the third floor has blabbed on me yet," she said, holding still while a seamstress adjusted the dress she was wearing. She looked like Kali the Hindu goddess of destruction with a flurry of arms around her shoulders and waist.

Grayson told his personal assistant Bryan to find one of the best designers in the city with the earliest availability, and as usual, he'd worked a miracle.

She was trying on a skin-tight tube dress that was blush-colored, and she looked, in his estimation, exquisite.

"It's barely been 72 hours, so there's still time... so far I like everything," he said looking up, to no one in particular, momentarily distracted from his laptop.

It didn't matter what they put on her, she looked amazing.

She often looked the opposite of what the outfit tried to convey. If the outfit was buttoned up and professional, it made her look buxom and dangerous. If it was bold and daring, she looked elegant and regal. In a simple, floating white dress she looked like smooth, dark temptation. If it was tacky or trashy, she simply elevated it. It was as though she was too much of a good thing, and no one knew a thing about designing for her.

"Y'all don't have any like... t-shirts and jeans?" she asked.

"I'm not paying for t-shirts and jeans," he said, the true meaning of his statement lost on their guests.

The two of them shared a look.

"What about pajamas," she ventured.

"Definitely not paying for pajamas," he said with a raised eyebrow, "but thank you for reminding me. You brought lingerie, correct?" he directed at the designer.

"Of course," she replied professionally. "It'll take a few days if you require a custom fit."

If the designer had an opinion, it was well hidden from everyone.

Amara stared at him staring intently at his laptop.

"Thought you were on vacation?" she pointed out.

"I'm not working; I'm writing a speech."

"Hit me," she said.

He scoffed. "It's not finished yet."

He was giving a commencement speech at MIT, at which time they would also be presenting him with an honorary degree.

After he opted for a GED instead of finishing out high school, he'd had another meltdown and was expected to work at a local grocery store in place of school. Instead, he spent mornings and afternoons at the library teaching himself whatever he wanted to learn, which was soothing beyond measure. That Spring he received his scholastic test results, which were near perfect scores. The college recruiters soon followed, and that fall he was off to MIT on a full scholarship.

He never graduated. He'd accepted a job at the NSA after hacking into their network. It was the most money he'd ever seen anyone make, at the time. So much for being a grocery store bagger.

"Don't you have people for this?" Amara asked.

"I'd hire a certain someone, but she apparently considers getting paid to write some form of torture?" he recalled. "Besides, I'm not a politician. What kind of wunderkind am I if I can't come up with my own ideas?"

"It's not about saying someone else's words," lifting her hair into a potential updo while looking at herself in the mirror. "Some people are just more gifted at bringing out what you actually want to convey."

"Be that as it may," he looked up at her, "I'm not reading you my speech."

Amara put up her hands in surrender. "Fine. I'll just be arm candy then."

He smiled and looked up, his midnight blue eyes devastating her. She stared back, letting herself be devastated, and a moment longer his eyes were drifting, she could only guess where. She chewed her bottom lip.

They were locked in a game of sexual chicken, neither of them looking away. The tension rose around them.

One of the younger assistants stifled a giggle.

Amara would not be outdone. Deep down, or rather, very obviously and on the surface, she wanted to make the papers again.

"You keep that up I'm gonna ruin this dress before you even buy it," she threatened.

"Well I certainly intend to." he shot back.

That got the seamstress' attention.

Grayson glanced back at his laptop, his poker face back in place. He really fucking liked Amara, he was realizing. He found himself wondering about her Myers-Briggs type all the time. She seemed to like him just as much, but honestly, he couldn't tell, which he also liked. Their chemistry was off the charts, and she was becoming well aware of her worth to him.

So far she was following a very typical pattern in the mistress phase. Except for the fact that with Amara, he was becoming very sick at the thought of her becoming attached to him. She mustn't do that. He cared about her well-being after this was over. And he was starting to fear that he might need to give himself the same pep talk.

The designer spoke up after a long bit of silence, "If there's nothing else?"

Grayson looked up, "My assistant Bryan will take care of you, thank you," he said.

"He already has. Have a good day sir."

They hustled and bustled like they were breaking down a scene in a high school play. Suddenly they were gone, as quietly as they came. Her new wardrobe was strewn about the living room as if the boutique had thrown up in it, albeit neatly.

She stood there looking at him; the only sound was the sound of his typing.

"How do I take this thing off?"

"Rule number one, you will not be removing any of your clothing. Let a man unwrap his own presents."

"I don't have any pants."

"Rule number two, pants impede access," he retorted.

She should be excited at his words, so why wasn't she?

Was the real Grayson really paying a million dollars to take away her independence? It just didn't seem real.

I guess this is why they say not to sleep with men for money.

She hadn't accounted for the fact that she may not be allowed to be herself for four weeks.

"No snarky remarks?" He looked up from his laptop. Amara in her beautiful one-of-a-kind dress looked... hurt?

He sighed. He typed a little more, finishing his thought before closing the laptop shut.

"Is this already too much for you? Because it's been barely 72 hours," he warned.

His tone was concerned, his words calloused. She went from hurt feelings to puzzlement.

Was this guy really that much of an asshole?

Dale had tried to warn her about him. That he was a bad person to fall for, a tough man to live with. She couldn't conceive of it then. But now...

Was the man she met at work wearing a mask, or was this the mask?

The man he was in bed could certainly be relied upon. That man had no agenda but their mutual pleasure.

Maybe it was good to have a reason to want this to be over. She could uncover the man he actually was and be grateful to be free of him. And still walk away with a payday.

The trouble was, the more they had sex the more she felt for him. And the more she felt for him, the easier it was for him to hurt her. He, on the other hand, seemed not to be affected at all. But then again, she hadn't been trying to hurt him.

"I'm just supposed to walk around the house all day like this?" she asked in disbelief.

"You don't have to walk around in anything you don't want to," he replied. So for the first week, she didn't.

She sometimes wore the lingerie, but it really wasn't made to stay on all day.

She was either naked or semi-naked most of the time, or wearing one of his discarded dress shirts or a vintage tee.

"What are you doing?" she asked him one afternoon.

Grayson didn't answer.

"I'm bored. Are you bored?"

"No," he said.

"I don't believe you. Let's do something."

He shrugged slightly. "I'm all ears."

"Let's play hide and seek."

Grayson let out a little chuckle.

"When's the last time you played that?" she enthusiastically inquired.

"I'm afraid I wasn't very good with the concept," he reminisced. "And a bit too good at hiding."

"You mean to tell me you've never played hide and seek as an adult?"

The corners of his mouth went down. "Is that so odd?"

"It is when you're a billionaire and your house has 18 rooms," Amara insisted, somewhat outraged.

"22."

"You mean to tell me you've never brought a group of hoes here, got 'em drunk, and let 'em try and find each other? What are you doing with your life, exactly?"

"Wasting it, apparently," he grinned.

"Well, it's a good thing I'm here," Amara said, putting away her phone and reaching around his shoulders. She put his computer in sleep mode and wrapped her arms around his neck.

"Come and find me," she whispered.

He sighed a party pooper's sigh.

"Come aaaaaaaahhhhhhhh," Amara whined. "It'll be fun, I promise."

"Our ideas of fun are at odds."

Amara did a little kid bop back and forth on her heels as she skillfully persuaded him.

"Come on let's play come on let's play come on let's play come on let's play come on let's play—"

"ALRIGHT," Grayson shouted over her. "ONE...TWO...THREE..."

Amara raced out of the room.

"Count to 20!" he faintly heard her instruction.

Grayson instead pressed the power button on his computer and resumed his work.

He did, however, open up the live feed to his security system in the corner, watching Amara drift from screen to screen around his house.

She darted this way and that, looking for more opportune places to hide, careful at every turn not to be seen.

He gave up trying to work, a goofy grin growing on his face while he watched her.

At one point he noticed that she was starting to shed clothes.

Toplessly, she abandoned the downstairs laundry room and left her underwear in the hallway.

She was leaving him a trail.

He continued to watch, mesmerized. It looked like she was headed toward the patio.

What the hell was she doing?

She found a killer hiding spot in the poolhouse, but she seemed to be worried that she'd hidden a bit too well. After a while, she abandoned that spot.

He could tell that she started to entertain the notion that he wasn't looking for her at all. As she stomped out of her hiding place completely naked, he couldn't help laughing.

She was headed back to his room.

Hastily he got up and hid in a hall closet before she could round the corner.

He heard her pass him and open the door leading to his room.

"You could've just said you didn't want to play..." he faintly heard her begin. Then silence.

He abandoned his hiding place and hid behind his bedroom door, waiting for her to retreat back up the stairs.

Her footsteps grew closer and closer, no air of trepidation in them. He grinned.

She was right. This was fun.

Predictably, she got to the top of the stairs and began to retrace her steps, not even looking in his direction. By the time she turned around he was already braced to grab her and toss her over his shoulder, which he did.

Amara released a long, adrenaline-laced scream that rang through the hollow halls of the great house.

* * *

As he and Amara lay in bed, spent after another night of intense lovemaking, she looked unashamedly at him, at his elegant, chiseled features. She brushed his pale face against the skin of her hand, dark as a shadow in the moonlit bedroom. She could tell he was pensive and the moment was so perfect that she hadn't realized how quiet her mind had gone.

Grayson stared at the ceiling, engaging the numbers in his mind that crowded his subconscious. It was like a basket of files that got too high if left unattended. He added them together, then multiplied them. They subsided. It was the only thing that kept them at bay, like a never-ending game of arithmetic Tetris.

A question entered his mind that he would've swallowed if he was with someone else. He wouldn't have entertained the thought at all with someone else. Probably because he wouldn't need to— he would've already known the answer. He would've looked down and smiled absently at whoever was lying next to him, initiating a kiss rather than conversation.

"Do you think you would have been my friend in high school?" his voice broke through the blue-black night.

Amara huffed air through her nose as she lay across his chest, tickled by the sudden ask. The image was almost too hilarious.

"I think I probably would've tried horribly, and then you would've responded equally as horribly."

He grinned. "What do you mean?"

"I mean, I probably would've been in one of your classes or something, probably would've been... intrigued by you."

"Just a caveat— I was a fat kid with bad acne on anti-psychotic meds," he said.

"Yeah, I know. We all went to school with that kid Grayson," she scoffed.

He stiffened a bit, hopefully imperceptibly. "And that kid was a friend of yours?"

"No, but only because I was pretty much afraid of my own shadow in high school. If I hadn't met Mya and Kim I would've probably *been* you."

"So the answer is basically 'no' then."

"Well like I said, I would've probably been intrigued by you," she mused. "Probably somewhat intimidated. You're the kind of kid that I would wonder about, and then some serendipitous event would happen where we'd be forced to talk to each other. Lab partners in biology. Assigned seats on a field trip."

"I think I would've been... mean to you. Rude, rather. And secretly stealing looks at your body."

"Good luck with that one. My standard uniform was a giant oversized jacket and frickin' men's dress shirts."

Grayson snickered, thinking of bad high school fashion.

"What the hell were you thinking?"

"I really thought I was sexy in them," Amara giggled.

"You probably were. You're sexy in mine."

"Once I would've seen that your iPod was full of gangster rap, we would've definitely been friends."

"I think you mean my Walkman. Once you saw that my Walkman was full of one CD."

"Oh yeah, I forget that you're old," she giggled.

"I'm not old, you're young," he smiled.

"How did you do book reports without the internet?"

"Books."

"How did you check Webster at school? Oh, that's right, you didn't. Because it hadn't been invented yet. By you."

"Thank goodness we at least had the light bulb. And the horseless carriage."

"I can't believe that you...*created* Webster."

"I can't believe it either."

"I can't believe I'm fucking the creator of Webster."

"Pinch yourself, girl," he said.

She did. On the nipple, and he sucked in a breath. Amara giggled.

The next day was Friday, the first week coming to a close. Grayson woke to the muffled sounds of a gospel choir, a song playing through his beta-tested virtual assistant that Webster was developing. Dale was convinced that it could never get made. A little too "Big Brother" he'd said. But the collective memory was short and society had too much of a hard-on for unnecessary conveniences. After ten years, they were closer than ever to a prototype, confident they could beat Magellan, their biggest rival, to market. If Amara could figure out how to use it, then they were closer than he thought. And if he could hear her music all the way from his bedroom then that meant it was loud as shit.

They were still confined to Grayson's ½ acre estate in the hills laying low while the media heat died down. Amara made breakfast burritos and left the kitchen in profound disarray, trying her hand at making every filling ingredient, including scratch-made tortillas.

Later that day, Amara asked Grayson to teach her how to drive his stick-shift convertible and he was surprisingly enthusiastic. He was a fantastic teacher. Patient, like a father teaching his sixteen-year-old the ropes. He never raised his voice or panicked when the car, worth four times her annual salary, spasmed and lurched like it was having an orgasm. To her credit, she only stalled out about 17 times. She followed up every sincere string of curses with a sincere apology.

"It's okay, cars were made to be broken," he jokingly guilted her.

"I'm so, so sorry."

"You said that."

"I didn't realize that I needed to do squats to drive a car."

"Your muscles get used to it."

They switched places, and he drove the car around back and across the lawn and parked. Behind the house, the view was mountains and trees. It was like being in another country. Amara was wearing the most casual thing she could find in her wardrobe, a lavender sundress and matching pumps that she toddled in. He spent most of the lesson watching her legs as she shifted gears, so any damage to his clutch was mostly his own fault.

"We should've brought snacks."

"We just ate," he giggled.

"That's not the point," she argued. She kicked off her pumps and stretched her long limbs across the front seat and over his lap. His hands began a familiar pilgrimage up and down her calves. His eyes darted to the journey ahead between her thighs, compulsively trying to catch a glimpse of the promised land.

"There's no eating in this car," he replied, daring her to excuse the pun. She did, eyeing him seductively.

"You'd let me tear up the engine but I can't spill mustard on your armrest?"

"That's correct."

Suddenly there was a call coming in from the futuristic dashboard. It was Dale.

Grayson soundlessly lifted his index finger to his mouth, giving her the "shh" signal. Grayson hit a button on the dashboard.

"This is Grayson," he generically answered.

"Hey."

"Hey."

"Are you in the car right now?"

"Yes."

"Is Amara with you?"

"No."

Dale paused.

"Really?"

"Really."

"So who's with you?"

"No one."

"Hey, Amara," Dale said, knowing Grayson well enough not to believe him.

"She's not in the car, bro."

"Okay, well your STD medication came in today bro. You need to come pick it up."

Amara threw her head back in soundless giggles at the two of them. They really needed their own show, she thought.

"Did I have that sent to headquarters?" Grayson asked, laughter faintly present in his voice.

"Yeah, you did. All kinds of creams and... sponges."

"Okay, I will fly all the way there to come get it. Anything else?"

"Her name's been released."

The two of them looked at each other. It was inevitable, but still. It made Amara uncomfortable. It meant that there was someone out there she knew that was willing to sell her out without telling her. It was a possibility she never before thought to entertain.

"By whom?"

"An anonymous source, naturally. Blog Trash was the first to publish it, apparently last night, but now it's everywhere."

"No legal action we could take, I suppose."

"Not a chance."

"So what now?"

"Everything's pretty calm so far, other than the fact that everyone here is only pretending to be working."

"Any publicity is good publicity."

"You're right, we were drowning in obscurity so, thanks. You want to release a statement or what?"

"How about, 'suck my dick?'"

"Cool. Does Amara know that you wet the bed until you were a fucking teenager?"

Grayson pursed his lips and shook his head slowly, inadvertently confirming it was true. That asshole. Dale was lucky he was 200 miles away. Amara covered her mouth as she doubled over in laughter.

"I'm busy I'll call you later," Grayson hastily said.

"Okay, dude. By the way, your grand wizard klan costume just came back from the cleaners, so I'll just leave here for you."

Amara's jaw dropped as she looked at him faux accusatory, and a bit turned on.

She was already sexy, so whenever she actually put her mind to being so, it turned him into a stammering idiot.

Amara's eyes traveled down his body and settled on his groin. So did her left foot. She locked eyes with his.

He probably wasn't really a klansman. But if he was, it was her civic duty to keep fucking him.

"Hello?" Dale was still on the line in the top-down convertible.

"Bro, I think she's into it," Grayson said, their eyes still meeting. Amara smirked.

"Bye Dale!" Amara shouted.

"No need to yell Amara, I can hear you," Dale assured her.

Grayson hit a different button on the dash and the call disappeared.

"You weren't supposed to hear that last part," Grayson said, looking morose.

Amara failed to stifle a smile as she licked her bottom lip. She knew what he was doing and it was adorable. She got down to brass tax.

"Got protection on you?"

He sighed a defeated sigh and hung his head.

He didn't, and the last thing he wanted to do was move. Amara gave him a 'tsk tsk' and removed her legs from their position across his lap.

"This was just supposed to be a driving lesson," he defended himself.

Amara simply relocated to the back seat.

"You should know better than that with me."

She produced two condom packets from her bra. He smiled.

"Has the top-down convertible taught you nothing?" she smirked, "always be prepared."

"I see I've taught you well," he said. The look in her eye was naked and carefree desire. He knew enough about women to know they only looked like that when there were feelings involved. He thought ahead to their inevitable fallout and nearly choked on the guilt.

"Your... future suitors will be very happy," he suddenly said.

"Um...yeah..." Amara said enthusiastically as she raised both eyebrows. The statement was totally weird and he didn't seem to notice. She tried to ignore it.

"You know," he continued as he joined her in the back seat, "purple just so happens to be my favorite color."

"Okay, now I feel like the klan thing is more for you than for me."

"Sorry, I made it weird."

"You did. And it was already weird."

"*Damn.* You seemed so into it," he lamented.

Amara laughed an infectious giggle. He smiled.

She hiked up her dress to straddle him, careful not to do any of the undressing herself. His big hands went to her thighs, then the fabric around her backside. He let out a contented sigh and she tried not to notice. She gazed at him for a while and put her hands in his dirty blond hair.

"Jeez, you are a bit... Aryan. How am I just now realizing that?"

He smiled. "You're color blind Amara. Congratulations."

"It's kind of making me uncomfortable."

"Care to time travel?" he raised an eyebrow, "I know a little bit of German."

"*Fuuuck*, you want it bad, don't you?" Amara was immediately aggressive in responsive.

Grayson's heartbeat accelerated at a dangerous speed and he was instantly breathless. Holy shit, she was hot. He kept forgetting that he wasn't entirely used to it. He couldn't talk so he just nodded.

He was a bit in over his head, as he didn't know enough German to make it dirty.

But she didn't know that.

He improvised.

11

Chapter 11

"Slavery," Mya merely said when Amara finally got around to her girls again later that week. She had quite a bit to catch them up on.

"He's a man, Mya," Kim said. "Ignore her, girl that shit is way hot."

"The sex is... next level," Amara added.

"How would you know, *virgin*," Kim chided.

"Oh, I don't know, how many times do *you* usually come in a night?" Amara bragged.

"Oop!" Kim simply exclaimed, admitting defeat.

"Slavery," Mya repeated, not letting the subject die.

Amara scoffed. "What am I supposed to do? We can't leave, the press knows my name now, we'll get mobbed."

"It wasn't me," Kim needlessly confessed.

"You think if you weren't there, if it was just him, he'd be holed up in his house like that? You think if you were wifey, he couldn't call a damn helicopter to come get y'all and zip you to... wherever??"

Mya's words chipped away at her ego.

It was entirely possible she was being played, but she couldn't figure out why or to what end. Was this really some bizarro Misery re-enactment? Why wouldn't he just be honest with her?

He was brutally so about their arrangement as it was. That and the volatile way he could melt her heart one moment and punch it the next had her wanting to pack her bags before it got any worse, damn the money.

But then...what would she do?

If she up and left him he'd resent her for sure, maybe go all power trip on her and blackball her around town.

He's not like that, she tried to assure herself.

Don't be your mother, she countered.

She was convinced that she simply couldn't know for sure. She had no choice but to stay.

There were plenty of perks to keep her buoyant for another three weeks. Like his mouth, for one.

"Whatever," Amara dismissed, feeling cold. "Slavery or none, I agreed to four weeks. Eyes on the prize, ladies."

They had another gourmet meal by candlelight that evening, courtesy of a personal chef on loan to him from a mere millionaire, the owner of a small trendy airline. Nothing like stuffed duck breast to lift a girl's spirits.

She did, however, eat her dinner in silence.

"You're mad at me," he suddenly said.

Sensitive Grayson was back, she thought.

Amara shrugged. "It's not that deep," she dismissed. "Just thinking about something Mya said today."

"The friend that hates me."

"That's the one."

"Enlighten me."

She sighed. "You don't wanna hear."

"Your silence is frightening enough. Go ahead; I won't break."

"Basically... she keeps bringing this whole arrangement back to slavery."

His big blue eyes were like planets in front of the candlelight. They were thoughtful.

"Isn't slavery by definition unpaid?"

"Which is always Kim's point," Amara interjected, "but Mya is more looking at... the gestalt of it."

He sat back in his chair. "Amara, your vocabulary gives me a boner."

"See, that right there. Mya would kick your ass if she were here."

He huffed a laugh, his mouth full of food.

"I shouldn't be turned on by your intelligence?" he took a sip of wine as he looked at her, giving her the smolder. It wasn't studied, it was real. Her eyes moved to his Adam's apple, which she always found gross when they were too pronounced but his was beautiful.

Amara managed to continue, though she was now aggressively thinking about sex. "The implication is that an African American woman with a large vocabulary is sooo rare— 'exotic' to use your word— that to come across it causes your circuits to overload."

"Is your friend also a virgin?" he psychically predicted.

Amara smirked. "As far as I know," she admitted.

"You're like a flock of geese," he said smiling.

Amara laughed.

"There she is," he said.

No, there you *are*, she thought. When he talked like that it felt like they were a couple. It was a sweet nanosecond that she tried not to savor.

"Oh, I'm not done, hotshot," she challenged.

Grayson made a summoning motion with his hand.

"She really took issue with the idea of me walking around half-naked every day."

"Ah."

"Because on some plantations slaves were only allotted a stark amount of clothing a year, and if they didn't make it last then they were made to walk around half-naked even in winter."

"Frederick Douglass," he said.

Amara looked at him, appreciative. She wanted to swipe everything off the table right then and there, and maybe she would have, but the chef and his two-man crew were still there cleaning up.

"I've read a few books in my life, Amara," he retorted, refusing to be flattered.

After a moment he continued.

"I don't know what to say to that, or what you want me to say. I would say

'You're free to leave,' but it's not as though I feel the need to prove that I'm not, in fact, a slavemaster. Is that what you think of me?"

Aw man, now he was feeling guilty. He probably wouldn't let her go down on him now as she wanted.

"It's not about what I think of you, it's about what I think of me," she assured him.

Another silence.

"And if we're being honest, I really can't say 'you're free to leave,' because contracts go both ways, Amara," he blurted out, sounding agitated.

"No one said anything about leaving," she eased. He had a panicky energy, and he was quiet. He seemed to be wondering how long she'd been feeling this way, and it was quickly becoming exaggerated.

"I didn't peg you for the type that's constantly bringing up slavery," he couldn't help adding.

Yikes. He was turning on her.

Amara's eyes went wide. She wasn't worried about his feelings anymore. Which was perhaps a good thing because gentleness seemed to agitate him further.

"Well, first of all, I don't, and secondly, if you had your listening ears on, I said Mya brought it up, not me. Of course, I like, that *you* like, that I'm naked all the time. It makes me feel very sexy."

The cleaning commotion in the kitchen seemed to get louder as if to remind them that other people were privy to their conversation.

His demeanor softened. She continued.

"But do I think it could be construed by someone on the outside as a little creepy? Yes. I mean, I get slavery was a long time ago, but it's a bit like if your great great grandma got kidnapped by Pennywise the clown alien when she was a kid. Sure it was a long time ago, but if clowns kept coincidentally showing up in your gutters generations later, it would be stupid not to be suspicious."

He was silent again for a spell, calm again as he said, "I'm Pennywise the clown alien?"

"No, slave owners are the clown alien. You would be one of the subsequent clowns that followed," Amara laughed.

"One that is, supposedly, not related at all to the initial alien clown incident," he clarified.

"Right."

He looked across the table at her after a thoughtful moment.

"...You're right, that's totally sketch," he said. Amara giggled.

"Now imagine said clown was offended to his core that you would ever suspect he was there to eat your fear."

"Your entire life is a psychological thriller right now," he sympathized with a grin.

"And that's why Mya hates you," she smiled.

"Now I hate me," he said.

"Aww," she laughed, covering his hand with her own.

When he looked down at her hand, she quickly withdrew it, focusing on the task of pouring more wine into her glass. He watched her carefully as he said, "We were gonna venture out, eventually. Obviously. It just... snowballed so quickly."

"Can't we just... get whisked away in a helicopter somewhere?" she suggested, remembering Mya's words.

"Where? I have 500 million connects, globally. I've always wanted to go to Antarctica, but it doesn't seem like your kind of place."

"Oh my God, why do rich white people love Antarctica," she half-joked.

"And I've got one day to finish this confounded speech, but you walking around half-naked is incredibly distracting—"

"Would you let me see the damn speech," she insisted.

Grayson didn't want Amara seeing his heartfelt, idealistic words about stopping bullying forever on planet Earth, because he was sure Amara saw down to his marrow like an x-ray, and it was excruciating. In fact, he was never more aware of that fat ugly teenager with bad acne than when she was looking at him. But, he simply had no strength left to turn down another pair of eyes.

"Fine," he said.

Besides the rearranging and fleshing out of a few paragraphs, Amara had to do very little to Grayson's speech. He was an eloquent, learned man no doubt about that. But it was a bit too clinical to be about the optimistic future of a world without bullying, and it contained nothing of his sense of humor, which explained why he struggled with it so long. Once he was satisfied with it he sent it off to his assistant, and his mind was free to focus on... other things.

They had sex on the terrace in front of a fire that wasn't warranted in summer, but it was romantic, and as she predicted, he'd stopped her when she tried to give him oral sex. They lay under the duvet from the bed, for which the weather was also too hot.

"I wish I could be there to see you give the speech," she told him.

"You can watch it online," he consoled her, his eyes closed.

"Yeah..." she replied.

"You'd just make me nervous," he made the excuse.

Amara was silent.

He was starting to hear her voice in his head.

"The story will go spiraling out of control if you show up there," he appealed to reason.

"Because it's doing so well now," she dug sarcastically.

"We're not trying to improve it; we're trying to choke the life out of it," he protested. Did she think he was purposely holding back on a better solution? Why did he care so intensely what she thought about what *he* thought, he wondered.

"Only problem is, the more you deny something is happening, the more you fuel it," she offered.

"Is there a better idea in my future?" he sniped.

"As a matter of fact, smartass, there is," she shot back.

A potent rush of blood hit his groin.

"Hit me," he said, using her vocabulary.

"Give the people what they want."

It sounded like a terrible idea of course, but he played along.

"I'm listening..."

"You're a billionaire, dating one of your lowest employees, who happens to be black. When everyone knows blondes from other countries are your m.o."

The fire danced along her sharp features. She tucked her hair behind her ear adorably.

When he was stone-faced, she continued, "People are allowed to be intrigued. It's kind of a cool story if we're being honest. People always equate this type of thing to Cinderella."

She stopped to see if he was following her, but apparently, he wasn't, because he'd locked onto a single word, the fourth one she'd said.

"'Dating…'" he quoted.

Amara sighed and rolled exasperated eyes, "In the public's eyes, you know what I mean."

"And when it's over in three weeks I'll never live it down," he predicted.

It seemed to her that he was bashing her over the head with it.

"Not if they're already tired of it before then," she posited.

"So I should just feed you to the press?" he concluded.

"Forget the press; you're the CEO of Webster for goodness sake. You should be the poster child for oversharing."

"…Post every waking moment on Webster?" he said.

Amara nodded. "Share our half-eaten breakfast."

"Water directly from the source," he agreed, the idea slowly dawning.

"Blow those grainy photos into oblivion; they'll be worthless."

"They'd have no choice but to go away. Maybe not completely but…" He looked down at Amara, and she thought he was going to call her a genius, but instead, he said, "You know, if I weren't so distracted, I would've thought of this myself."

Amara stroked the fine hairs of the arm cradling her head.

"Jeez, you're sexist too?" she ribbed, smiling.

12

Chapter 12

Two weeks into their arrangement, Grayson realized his second mistake, which was carrying on their affair at his personal estate.

If it were anyone else, there would be no problem, because she would've likely spent very little time there. But they would've had no privacy anywhere else, thanks to his first mistake. And now that they'd been holed up there, his house was covered in her essence. Her smell after a bath bomb, the floral scent that usually nauseated him but smelled like the garden of Eden on her. Her eclectic music playlist wafting through the kitchen while she trashed it making breakfast, or baking bread, which she was quite good at, or venturing on some elaborate french dish she'd never before dared to attempt. It never looked like the picture, but it always tasted great. The sound of her trying to get his smart house to talk back to her like it was an actual person, and her curse-filled rants as she failed, most of the time.

She'd now had the most access to him than any woman had ever had, perhaps counting his own mom even. She had inadvertently grown on him. Moving on from her was now going to be exponentially more difficult. She roamed the house like a half-naked ghost while he worked, because an entirely work-free vacation was wishful thinking.

Sometimes she sat quietly in his room with her headphones in, listening to podcasts or going down pop culture rabbit holes, watching videos on MeTv.

But he did often take breaks. Erotic ones.

She liked to message him wild things on Webster while they were in the same room.

He would look over at her, and she would be watching something, looking completely oblivious. Then he would send something back that would shock his poor saintly mother into the afterlife, and he felt her energy heighten behind him. Sometimes they would wait and let the tension linger. Most times they didn't.

Amara was working too. She became their social media czar, and it was indeed a full-time job. Documenting their every mundane moment, posting and tagging and posing as both of them. Her attempts to post things in his voice almost never failed to make him laugh.

The plan to become the nauseating couple on Webster got rid of the feeding frenzy, but it created another problem. Apparently, there was a celebrity couple vacuum, and Grayson Davis and Amara Riley were filling the void.

By the end of the second week, the media had given them the nickname "Gramara."

Grayson was none too pleased.

"I was really rooting for 'Amayson,' Amara said from her side of the bed. Grayson was up working at his desk.

"It's getting away from us," he prophesied.

"Let the beast do its job," said Amara sleepily.

She was starting to get used to her wardrobe. She was wearing a fancy satin pale pink dress that she thought would make a decent nightgown. Turns out it actually was a nightgown.

That night was to be their first public appearance. A movie premiere that he'd planned on skipping, but it was a convenient way to gauge the success of their social media experiment. Plus, once Grayson saw Amara's face light up at the suggestion of dinner and a movie, he knew it was going to happen.

Grayson was a nervous wreck.

"There are a lot of weirdos out there," he alluded.

There had already been five Webster pages dedicated to killing Amara Riley that had to be taken down.

Five seemed like a lot to her.

Grayson had a pretty intense row with Dale on the phone about it, who insisted they didn't have grounds to press charges after talking to the lawyers.

"Amanda was probably behind at least one of those," Amara joked. Grayson hadn't laughed.

She was afraid he would change his mind about letting them leave.

"You said you hired security," she reminded him.

Grayson sighed and lowered his head.

"If I would've known this would turn my life into a circus..."

Amara was silent.

She wasn't worth the hassle.

It'd been a while since she'd heard a callous word from him, but when she did it was always about the "arrangement." He seemed to regret it endlessly, that is when he wasn't reaping the benefits.

She, however, was having the hiatus of a lifetime. She was sort of itching to get back to her life, oddly. She planned to keep her lifestyle virtually the same while she invested the crap out of her money and she was excited about it. She came by it relatively easily and tried to use that attitude to keep her in the mood to take risks and not just hoard it. Of course, she would diversify between high and low risk. She had her eye on real estate for the high-risk investment.

Yes, she did hope that he would still be in her life, if only as friends. But in the event Grayson made a calculated attempt to avoid her for life, she wanted to fill her world with enough excitement that she would be fine.

The energy in the room had plummeted while Amara was lost in thought, and she wondered if he thought she was angry at him. As Grayson kept his back to her, she felt his contrition about the stinging words, his inward struggle between making amends and staving off emotion. Should she put him at ease?

"If you would've just put the damn top-up," she accused, reminding him of their first kiss.

He swirled around in his chair with a glare, a grin of recollection on his mouth.

Sweet mother of mercy, he was a sex monster.

But then again, so was she, she was beginning to notice.

She shot him a look brimming with attitude and burning through him from all the way across the room.

She looked pissed, so he wanted her.

"Come here," he said, as was his custom.

"No," she simply said, getting out of bed. "I'm taking a shower."

"We have an arrangement," he reminded her from his chair, ratcheting up his rich jerk routine. He attempted to clasp her hand as she passed but she snatched it away, upping the ante.

"Fuck the arrangement, I'm dirty, and I need a shower," she stated matter of factly, rounding the corner to the bathroom. Her heavy satin nightgown quickly fell with the slight pivot of her bronze shoulders.

Opening the glass shower door, she shut on the water with a smirk. She fiddled around with the temperature a moment, and before she could turn around Grayson had snuck up behind her and dug his long fingers into her soft middle.

She shrieked and laughed where his touch was inadvertently tickling her.

"Are you kidding me right now?" he quietly breathed in her ear. He'd shed his silk pajama bottoms, and his erection was teasing her lower back.

Damn, he wanted her, she thought. It sent a rush through her that forced her eyes tightly shut.

Her head flew back, rooting around for his kiss. Her eyes slowly opened as if waking from sleep. He was looking at her.

"Kiss me," she panted.

"No," he said.

He was punishing her for her impudence.

More importantly, if he kissed her, he knew what would happen. Amara's kiss was a vortex, and he had to be careful where he opened it. He made out with her incessantly, and each time he inadvertently became like a newborn at his mother's breast, sometimes at the expense of Amara who'd be just as lost and writhing around for his...anything.

Amara's tongue slithered out, and he couldn't resist meeting it. They lapped and pecked, putting off further touching, letting their lips do all of the deliciously tedious work. He engulfed her whole mouth stealing a moan from her throat. Desire was at a low boil in his blood, but Grayson steeled his resolve, and they finished each other off unconventionally, doing their best in between to use the shower as the manufacturer intended.

He felt himself getting lazier and lazier about condoms as it was. He knew she wasn't fertile. Because there was an app for that and he was, unapologetically, a weirdo. Still. These things weren't exact.

A few hours later the glam squad arrived. Amara gained a few instant fans in the makeup crew, which by mid-afternoon had no trouble yelling at her to hold still a few dozen times as though they'd known each other forever.

Grayson was dressed elegantly yet casual in a blazer with a very small black and white houndstooth print so that it was barely noticeable and just looked grey from afar. His hair was cut with the top kept long and slicked back, highlighted with blond that made his eyes supernaturally blue and expressive.

James Dean was now the much uglier brother they kept in the basement.

He looked trendier than she was used to, like every penny of his billions.

For the first time in a long time, she was wishing that she could simply be blonde and white and unquestionably suited to him. Was she really going to put herself under all that scrutiny reserved for the deservedly talented and famous? She hadn't seen herself yet, and she couldn't judge by his expression as they sat across from each other.

Naturally, he was done before her, and he didn't even bother to look in a mirror. She asked him to take a photo for their carefully crafted Webster pages, but instead of taking a picture, he made the team start over.

"It's too heavy," he insisted, referring to the carefully contoured mask of foundation and shimmering ombre effect of her eyelids. She looked beautiful, glamorous even, but to him, she looked like a stranger.

"This is going to last all day, and it'll hold up for the cameras," the lead artist defended.

"I don't care about that," he said. "Just make it look like she's not trying. At all."

"He's saying I'm a schlub," Amara quipped. She needed all the help she could get, she thought. Why was he trying to humiliate her?

"No, he means 'effortless,'" the artist gleamed as if trying not to give something away.

After her makeup was corrected, they dressed her in a navy and white striped boatneck midi dress with cropped sleeves. Her locs were arranged in an elaborate off-center bun. The modest jewelry on her neck and wrists glittered.

"I look like a black Kennedy," she said, looking at herself in the mirror.

"Amy, you were born in the 90's. Act like it," he retorted, as they locked arms and made their way to the chauffeured car.

He had taken to calling her Amy in private, and suddenly the name had gone from a career concession to the sacred omen of his burgeoning feelings for her.

The sex had already become more and more like lovemaking, where the pet name got its start. She tried not to draw attention to it, lest he feel the need to censor himself.

The two were unable to keep a low profile at the premiere. Grayson was just one of the financiers, but when they showed up, the flashbulbs went off as though they were one of the stars. Amara's arm tightly clasped Grayson's on the blood-red carpet, and while he was a bit taken aback as well by their enthusiasm, his composure was miles ahead of hers.

Grayson's assistant Bryan had found them the scariest, most professionally presented human pit bulls that money could buy, so she wasn't afraid for her safety. When Amara heard her name for the first time, coming from the great blinding bushel of photographers a few meters away, she mouthed "Oh my God" in an exaggerated fashion, somewhat forgetting that they could plainly see her and were intentionally observing her. They found her naivete amusing and murmured laughter at her reaction.

"Yeah, we know your name, hon," she heard from the amorphous camera blob.

The more she heard her name, the more she hid behind Grayson's right shoulder.

"You didn't give her any media training Davis?" one of them anonymously barbed.

Grayson's jaw had already become tightly clenched, and he was about to let his agitation show.

After all these years he could still recognize a bully, no matter their station. Like a shark detecting blood in an ocean, his instincts to devour became acute. Unlike sharks, however, their bloody metallic scent wasn't a draw— it made him want to vomit.

"We've been busy," he suddenly heard Amara respond. The crowd chuckled.

"Doing what?" the blob distantly asked.

"What?" Amara strained to hear.

"Doing what?" the blob echoed, more voices this time.

"Oh," she nodded. "Having sex," she made sure to project.

The camera mob erupted in laughter.

She looked at Grayson in time to see his now patented look of disapproval mixed with amusement. She shrugged and furrowed her brow with an expressive look of "what, like they don't know?"

When they got further down the carpet towards the venue, popular actress Sharon Adams was there, who was short with long red hair and pale green eyes.

She wasn't in the movie, perhaps a guest of someone else, but when she saw Amara, she instantly came toward her and held out both her hands for Amara to grab.

Sharon had been at the Malibu party, and while Amara felt like they hit it off in a Hollywood kind of way, she was surprised yet grateful to be a recipient of such warmth, though she was still wary that it was Hollywood warmth.

Whatevs. She wasn't here to climb ladders; she was technically on the highest fucking rung. At least for the next two weeks. The paparazzi went into a frenzy as they greeted each other.

"Grayson, what were you thinking bringing a normal person to a premiere?" she joked in Grayson's direction.

Okay, so they've slept together, Amara thought definitively. Amara noticed that sex had given her some newfound powers of perception she wasn't sure she wanted.

"She doesn't seem to need my help," he answered drily as they exchanged side kisses.

"How are you holding up so far?" Sharon asked.

"Girl, I am *rocking this*," Amara exaggerated. Sharon laughed. She even elicited a laugh from Grayson. Except Grayson's seemed more like a laugh-to-keep-from-crying response.

They entered through the grand double doors and were seated in a small theatre next to some other unfamous muckety mucks rather than the famous ones, save for the director. She never thought much of the director, but had much more sympathy for him and others of his ilk, after she sensed flames of financial and professional pressure that must've been lapping his face while the movie played.

When it was time for dinner, they emptied out of the theater to an auditorium draped in white and red cloth decor, filled with white tables large enough to seat eight, each with elaborate rose centerpieces.

Grayson was in no mood to socialize, so they accommodated him on the spot setting up a table for two near the low light of the hallway that led to the kitchens. He seemed not to be bothered by the fact that everyone knew he was basically telling them to bugger off, but as he was richer than all of them, and they were in Hollywood, they did their damndest not to let any annoying etiquette violations show.

Amara's post-sex perception (PSP?) senses were telling her that she was in the company of other highly paid companions, and they seemed to sense the same about her. She wished she could project the opposite, but obviously, she couldn't.

Well, this feels horrible, she inwardly lamented. She tried to console herself with the idea that she was likely the highest paid, and certainly the highest educated. Perhaps in history. But when she did, it was almost as if the need to feel superior had blackened her heart.

However savvy she'd tried to be with her financial scheme, she'd indeed been naive about the emotional fallout, just as he'd predicted.

He'd tried to tell you, Amara considered herself with pity.

On some level, she felt a bit ungrateful for complaining about her reasonably successful foray into prostitution. How many of these other women had to climb some sort of seedy ladder to get to where she was now? Yet while these women had likely made their life choice consciously, Amara was waffling, pretending. Grayson picked up on her mood.

"You seem... melancholy Amara," he commented, radiating unrelenting, brooding gorgeousness. She couldn't feel more unworthy. She was glad he made her take off the heavy makeup, it would've been like lipstick on a pig.

"Do you feel the prostitute vibes around us?" she said.

Grayson slowly broke out into another killer smile.

"We've got to get you some whispering lessons," he mused.

"I am a part of their numbers," she admitted in a low voice as she elegantly skewered another bite of perfectly cooked New York strip.

"You are," he replied, failing to mince words. "Does it bother you?"

Her eyes briefly widened. She didn't answer; she simply scoffed and continued to eat in silence. She was clearly on the verge of tears. Her perfectly coiffed hair and flawless makeup made her crumbling expression particularly heartbreaking. In an effort to blink away a clinging tear, it instead fell.

Grayson's heart was in an unforgiving vice. He wanted to tell her that he would've been honored to take her to dinner and a movie without a contract, that her presence had made an otherwise vapid and unbearable event exciting and endearing— almost like a first date, which he wasn't sure he'd ever really had.

But he couldn't, because this wasn't a relationship, and he wasn't entirely sure it would've helped in the present circumstances.

Because the reality was she had prostituted herself. For him and only him, he was pretty sure. And now she was confronting the consequences of her naive decision. The vice grew unbearable.

Even he knew that she probably wouldn't want to hear that she could've made it here on her own merits. He instead stuck with what he knew, with the language of the contract.

"When we get home I'd like to pleasure you until you forget about this unpleasantness," he attempted to console her.

He was looking directly at her, she knew, even though she was staring at the inside of her wine glass as she took a drink.

Like any decent prostitute, Amara too had found her drug of choice.

She put her elbow on the table, her hand on her chin. She discreetly took her shoe off and searched until she found his leg under the table. Grayson's signature poker face was in place.

"Mable, Mable," he said.

Amara suddenly perked up.

"My Grandma used to say that! Where are your people from? That's a very specific regionalism."

Grayson sucked his breath audibly through his teeth and gave her a sultry stare. Amara huffed a laugh and slowly shook her head. He was trying to cheer her up, she realized. The gesture itself had worked.

"Say 'vernacular,'" he said.

"You're completely ridiculous," she replied.

"Say it."

Amara's foot ventured further up the leg it found.

"Vernacular," she said, tossing her head to one side, exposing her smooth neck.

He smiled as he looked down at her lips.

"Use it in a sentence, girl," he used his bedroom voice that never failed to turn her on, but she couldn't help bursting out laughing.

He eyed her carefully as her laughter rang out in the makeshift dining room causing heads to turn, a foreign pain growing in his cheeks from smiling.

13

Chapter 13

By the third week, he was breaking all kinds of cardinal rules. He got dangerously sloppy about the condoms, to the point she would have to remind him and he would act irritated.

"Are you seriously pissy because I asked you to put on a condom?"

"No," he insisted, resuming his thrusting posture once the rubber was in place.

"Grayson... you're literally inside me, you think I can't tell that you're irritated?"

"If you can tell, then I wish you'd be quiet."

Amara gave him a stank face. "Bro, I wanna come too, alright? I'm just trying to help you stick to your 80/20 plan."

"I'm perfectly capable of worrying about it myself, Amy, *Jesus.*"

"Well, you're not the only person it would affect," she scoffed.

Grayson rolled his eyes in the semi-dark. "Yes, I'm sure you're very concerned about landing your dream gig."

He was being cynical but Amara just smiled. "And what dream gig is that?"

Grayson hid his own smile with kisses down her neck.

"You want my cum and you know it," he teased in her ear.

Not to be outdone Amara looked him square in the eye as she whispered, "You wanna give it to me and you know it."

He nodded once. He was rock hard in record time but tried to hold off his release as long as possible. It was Grayson's turn to feel the butterflies at Amara's unflinching lustful stare. They locked eyes and barely moved, grinding slowly against each other as they quietly moaned and dirty-talked the paint off the walls.

She started to notice he had a jealous streak, an irrational one. Especially when it came to Dale. He obviously had no intention of letting Amara and Dale cross paths again. An irrational impulse made worse whenever Amara asked after him. Even something as innocent as a "What did he say?" while Grayson casually recalled one of their conversations was enough to unsettle him.

Jealousy meant he cared, right? She shuttered, a chillingly familiar ring to her words.

She'd discovered the true extent of it the hard way, at a dinner party Dale was throwing at his house in South San Francisco.

It was more of a very relaxed business dinner with the guest of honor being Bel Hafiz, the founder of MeTV. Another young 30-something billionaire who'd revolutionized the world nine years ago with his ambitious side project. They all used to work together at Magellan before it became the search engine conglomerate it is today. They were discussing the prospect of merging in some way, trying to predict the technological trends for the next decade. It was also partially a blind date for Hafiz, set up by Dale's own new matchmaking girlfriend Avery.

Amara was surprised to see that Dale had a Spanish-style hacienda for a home. She thought for sure he'd have some space-age minimalist cube out in the desert somewhere. But instead, it was in the middle of a lush green wood that masked the sight of the nearby beach, but not the sound. It had beautiful white stucco columns and a dark reddish-brown clay roof. The vast courtyard seemed somehow quaint. Staircases decorated with colorful hand-painted tiles led to various villas that lined the courtyard's border. Indoors it had every modernity, and when they retreated to the courtyard in the evening, it was like being transported.

"How are you coping with celebrity, Amara?" Dale began, somewhat facetious.

"Seeing as how I've been cooped up at the Davis compound for three weeks

I'd say pretty well."

"The story's going to outlive the relationship, I'm afraid," Grayson ruthlessly assessed.

Both Dale and Bel went rigid, but Amara just lobbed Grayson in the arm as if she had no intentions of being temporary.

"I think I've been hit harder by puppies," he said dryly.

"And I have no doubt you made a puppy feel like it needed to hit you," Amara said just as dry. The company laughed.

"How long have you been growing yours?" Bel asked Amara.

Both Amara and Bel had their hair in locs. Bel's were thicker but his hair finer. They lay like majestic vines down to the middle of his back when they were pulled back and secured. Bel was Middle Eastern, but he looked to Amara as though he was African American but very light-skinned. He was handsome with stunning grey eyes.

"Eleven years," she answered.

"They're beautiful," he said.

"Thanks," she continued. "The beginning stage was...rough. But my best friend Mya is a black hair magician."

"These two gave me so much shit when I started mine," Bel admitted.

Amara gave Dale and Grayson each a disapproving look.

"In all fairness, he was growing weed on our balcony at the time," Dale defended himself.

Amara laughed.

"Hey, that was my inspiration for MeTV so who's laughing now," Bel boasted.

"You know, I applied for a job at MeTV as soon as I graduated, and I did not get a callback," Amara volunteered, pretending to be offended.

"Just whoring yourself out to Silicon Valley, weren't you Amara?" Grayson suddenly piped up with a scoff. Dale's smiling expression froze as he just stared at him across the table.

"Basically," Amara replied, laughing off his remark. "I didn't know what I was going to do, I just knew something exciting was happening and I thought maybe if I get in on the ground floor, someone would let me be a part of it."

"MeTV had an IPO five years ago, Amy. I would hardly call that the ground floor," he needlessly corrected.

"Well I agree, *asshole*," Amara continued, turning slightly to Grayson's direction, "but in terms of public consciousness it was still very new, and the application process is a whole hell of a lot different now than it was then."

Amara turned back to the table. Bel was laughing and so was his blind date, after almost doing a spit take. Grayson was sipping a drink when Amara turned back to look at him, and their eyes met. Judging by their energy, they either resented each other or were about to have sex on the table right there in front of everyone. Perhaps both. Grayson had a familiar haze of desire in his eyes but was otherwise poker-faced as he chomped on a piece of ice.

"Davis, you gotta keep this one, bro," said Bel.

"He's gonna run her off," Dale tried to keep his tone light.

Amara ripped herself from his gaze and turned it back to the table.

"Takes a lot to run me off," Amara assured him.

"One million to be exact. After taxes," Grayson remarked.

Amara didn't look in his direction.

The conversation suffered a contextual hiccup and then continued. Amara focused her attention on her wine glass, twirling the stem so that the burgundy sloshed up the sides. She caught Dale's sympathetic gaze.

Amara froze.

God. He knew about the contract.

"Don't look at her," she heard Grayson's voice break in.

Amara's heart shifted into high gear, and for once it was not a good feeling.

"Dude... relax," Dale said exasperatedly.

"I'm fully relaxed, Dale. I'm saying don't look at her."

Dale looked at Grayson. The other girls at the table looked at Amara. The tension at the table rose, but Bel looked cool.

Dale was confrontational now. "What are you doing?"

"You gonna be her protector now?" Grayson suddenly blurted.

"Someone should," Dale retorted.

Dale's girlfriend Avery bristled. Amara was mortified.

Yep. He definitely knew about the contract.

Grayson smoothly got up from the table and sauntered back toward the house.

"Jesus," Bel said.

Dale looked over at Bel, a thousand words in his eyes. Bel shook his head with a snicker and took a sip of his drink.

"What on earth was that about?" Dale's girlfriend Avery wondered.

"Nothing. Just... Grayson," Bel said.

"Fucking Grayson, dude," Dale repeated, galled.

"He's gotta do it, bro, just let him," counseled Bel cryptically.

"No," Dale simply defied him, taking a drink.

The girls at the table had no idea what they were talking about, but Amara got yet another brief glimpse into their relationship. She wondered how Dale wasn't married yet and she was beginning to see that Grayson took up a great deal of his attention.

It stayed quiet another moment before Bel decided to take advantage of Grayson's absence.

"Bro, would you have guessed in a *million* years..."

Dale tried to catch on as Bel seemed to be secretive about his drift.

"You mean..." Dale nodded in Amara's direction.

Bel just smiled, and Dale continued cryptically as if no one else was there.

"Yeah, never in a million years."

Bel laughed with an intriguingly wicked sense of irony.

"Oh geez," Amara groaned, combing her fingers through her locs.

"You should've seen him at headquarters that day, dude."

"I heard about it," he said.

Amara's cheeks got warm. She was still floored that she could've been so memorable, but she wasn't hiding her face anymore. She shook her head as Dale continued.

"He was... creepy stalking her, like within the hour, dude."

Bel laughed with his eyes shut tight.

"Wait, what?" Amara stopped.

Dale just gave her a dismissive head shake as though it was too ridiculous to go into.

"He asked her 'do you wanna keep working here,' and she was like 'no thanks,'" Dale crudely summarized.

"That is not what I said," she assured Bel who gave her a playful jaw drop.

"That was pretty much all she needed to do, bro."

"And then you made me pretend to be dating you!" Amara exclaimed.

Bel was wide-eyed at that, and he looked over at Dale, who had taken a drink from his whiskey glass, just at the moment he realized he was desperate to recall the story. He was nodding wildly and huffing a laugh, squinting and pointing as the liquid burned his throat.

His girlfriend Avery gave him a disappointed groan.

"So I brought Amara to Malibu, right? His faaaaaaaaaace..." Dale ground out, and Bel was cracking up again at the visual.

"I paid Amara a thousand dollars right there on the spot," he added.

More laughter.

Amara was smiling as she cut through their laughter, "How is this funny, he is really pissed in there."

"That's his natural state, Amara," Bel broke the news.

"So I've noticed," she offered. She looked a little defeated.

"Listen, Amara. You remember what I told you on the plane?" Dale began.

That he's secretly a basket case and I shouldn't get my hopes up?

"Yeah," she simplified.

"Well, I was wrong. You seemed like a nice girl, and at the time, I didn't think you could handle his... moods. But now I think you might be the only one."

The statement tore her in two. It made her stomach flip-flop with hope, and yet it made her mentally cringe.

It was the same language her mother's in-laws used to keep her staying with her dad because the Rileys didn't do divorce. She was dismayed to find it just as persuasive to her own ears.

"Hardly," she answered Dale. "I know about the 80/20, and honestly I support it. His moods at 80 will be way worse than his shriveled up penis."

"He won't make it to 80 in his current state," Dale said ominously, with naked concern for his friend.

A shiver went through Amara's blood. What was he talking about? The party atmosphere threatened to change.

"It'll pass, they always do," Amara shrugged, trying to lighten the ambiance.

"This isn't a mood. I think he's on the verge of a meltdown. He's overdue..." Dale foreshadowed.

Then he lowered his voice to a whisper as if he knew Grayson had been listening but before now it had been of no consequence.

"I think he's in love with you, and it's freaking him out," he said.

The statement should've caused a heart attack, but instead, it felt like finding out you had a terminal illness.

She loved him that was true, but if he loved her then why did it feel like she was in jail? And if his love felt like jail, then there's no way this was the guy for her. She was worried about herself.

"Aww," Avery cooed, an encouraging hand shot out to touch Amara's wrist.

"And if that's the case then Amara," Dale continued, "I will pay you another five thousand dollars, every day, forever, if you stay with him," he bargained seriously. The table laughed.

"Dude that's like..." Bel began calculating, "she'll be a billionaire in ten years."

"Hmm, a billionaire??" Amara stroked a fake beard. "I don't know; he can be a real asshole."

"Please," Dale insisted. Amara laughed.

"Save us, Amara," Bel joked.

* * *

"While you were pouting in the kitchen, Bel offered me a job," Amara began after a wordless flight home in Grayson's jet.

Silence.

She was removing her pearl earrings and black spaghetti strap evening gown in her closet, safe from his gaze.

"You do know that I'm not attracted to Dale in any way," she continued, trying to start an adult conversation.

"Doesn't matter," Grayson replied. It was the closest she'd ever get to an admission of jealousy. She waited to see if he would continue. He didn't.

"Doesn't matter because you don't care, or doesn't matter because—"

"Exactly what I said," he clarified tersely.

"Babe, what you said doesn't make sense," Amara tried reasonably.

"It doesn't matter, because in a week this will be over and you're free to do what you want," he said resolutely.

"Good. Because you are insane," she sighed.

"You'll be a hot, sexy, millionaire, Amy. You might even make the cover of Jet."

"What the *fuck*, Grayson!"

"They'll probably give you an award."

"Are you drunk right now?"

"No, but it's an excellent idea."

It was suddenly silent in their room. He had indeed retreated upstairs while she was undressing. Amara appeared in the kitchen in a flowy silver negligee. He was drinking something brown and clear, pretending not to see her.

Really? Her having a job after their affair was over is driving him to drink? For some reason, the idea that she'd be of use to someone other than him seemed to send him over the edge. Was he angry that he may have to share a social circle with her now?

"For God's sake, Grayson, he's allowed to see something in me," she said.

"You've spent, what, an hour with Dale in your life? Jesus," he said, shaking his head, pouring himself another drink.

"I was talking about Bel," she corrected him.

"Oh, your other new best friend!"

Bel had taken to her as well he noticed, and the untamed vines of jealousy were now black and suffocating around his heart at the news he had offered her a job. He was completely irrational, he knew. Did he really expect her to never have another boss? Shouldn't he prefer that she worked for someone he knew and trusted? Or was it that he wouldn't be the one to explore her untapped potential?

"But back to that hour I've known Dale," she challenged. It was unsafe territory, but as he'd said, she only had a week left and didn't care anymore. "I'd love to give you some context, but you refuse to let me talk about that hour."

"I don't want to hear about how he paid you to blow him in business class," he said.

"That's right," Amara sarcastically conceded.

"I mean, the head is...spectacular, so I don't blame him. I don't blame you either, I blame myself, for not qualifying the virgin story fully."

"Nothing gets by you, Grayson," she deadpanned, turning to leave.

"What exactly is this magical position that you're so qualified for, I'm dying to know," he wondered aloud.

No way would she actually tell him so that he could crap on that too.

"Oh don't worry about that, it's nothing related to your boring snoozefest company."

"Oh, more blowjobs then," was the best he could come up with.

"You're not the only *billionaire* that can see I might actually be good at something," she stopped at the entrance to his downstairs bedroom.

"The only thing Bel can see that you're good at is draining my balls, and that I'm not in the mood to share," he replied.

She didn't want to say anything, because the abuse would continue. She also didn't want to be silent, in case he would try to sleep with her and bring up that stupid contract again, which she honestly couldn't wait to be free of. She decided to push him away with the truth.

"Maybe you should tell Dale that you resent him down to your core, instead of drinking yourself into a stupor."

"Foreshadowing!" he said enthusiastically. Grayson took another drink. "I love gothic literature, you know," he raised the tumbler to his lips again. "Is this the part where you give me all your Aunt Jemima wisdom after you've slept with me for a month?" he said before taking another drink.

Amara's pulse quickened. She would not be deterred. This dude was serving her some serious bullshit, and she fucking loved tennis.

"Yes! And then this is the part where you ignore very simple and obvious warnings, because you're a prideful clueless asshole, and then everyone looks on while you ruin your life with your own hands," she explained matter-of-factly.

He laughed, throwing his head back with a snort. He poured another drink. "You may very well be my soul mate, Amy. For another week at least."

"I'm going to bed, please don't try to touch me," she requested. She waited with bated breath for a retort that never came.

That night he didn't come back downstairs, and when she awoke that morning, she found him upstairs sleeping, still dressed, on the couch.

She woke him up unceremoniously.

"Wake up," she said. "We leave for Montenegro in an hour."

14

Chapter 14

Grayson's third mistake in as many weeks was the nail in the coffin. He was starting to make love to her on a regular basis.

He looked into her eyes. He twirled her hair around his fingers, he gave her nicknames. And generally tried to make her feel like she was his and only his.

It started out as a concession because as a rule, he didn't apologize.

He tried to express instead whatever negative emotion he felt in the moment about himself, and even then only when forced. He liked it that way because apologies tended to draw lawsuits.

When he was younger, he felt sorry for nothing, even when he was exploding in anger and destroying things. Every harsh word or gesture was a necessity of survival. He never apologized to Dale either, and they sometimes came to blows.

Now that they were older, they had an understanding. In his mind, time always did more than what apologies could ever do.

He tried to remember when he was so awful to a woman, but in his recollections of them, he didn't have any where he even talked to them. Aside from "Are you having a good time" or "More wine" or whatever else that made him sound like a waiter.

Paradoxically, there wasn't another woman he'd ever spent more time *not* talking to than Amara. And he loved that about her. That she could just be, there.

It was just his luck that he was incapable of wowing a woman that he actually liked.

Also, the fact that she felt contractually obligated to endure him made him want to vomit about, oh every five minutes.

It was only Amara herself that could make him forget.

So he made love to her.

Gave away pieces of his heart, the sorry consolation prize that it was. It seemed it was all he had left. She wasn't much interested in the money.

The fact that the more he'd done it, the less impressed she seemed to be, didn't help matters.

She couldn't even relax until he put on a condom, as though getting pregnant by him was a fate worse than death.

Not that he wanted a family, but he started to get clear visions of Amara as a mother, and in his mind, she was a good one.

No doubt it was all the lovemaking that caused his mind to take this perilous journey. It was as though all her best qualities seemed to culminate in the office of motherhood. Whatever progeny he was destined to have would be neurotic and spoiled and never know hard work, but with Amara as their mother, well. They just might have a chance.

What, did she think he would leave her destitute, to go through it alone?

Is it any wonder, the way she's treated? his inner voice protested.

Did she really think she could be more cautious about this than him?

She didn't trust him, and it hurt. He'd given her no reason, then again.

Clearly, the contract had been a terrible idea, one that hardly worked in his favor. He'd made a bad deal. Blinded by the sweet promise of poontang.

He was neither the first nor the last.

Yet if not for her quick thinking on the beach that night, he would've never had the best day of his life.

That is, before he royally ruined it.

While they were in the air on the way to Montenegro, he sat across from her, looking for traces of joy.

Things had indeed died down by then, and now they were jetsetting, like she wanted.

He couldn't find any traces of joy, however.

He could see the arch of her expressionless eyebrows slightly above the dark sunglasses she loved wearing, and her hair was kind of half up-half down and messy.

He'd flown in her best friend Mya to re-twist her hair before the party at Dale's, and he'd paid her handsomely for it.

Mya was darker than Amara and almost more striking. She was compact, small and petite, and seemed to float instead of walk like most professional dancers. She definitely still hated him. He was intrigued to find that he wasn't attracted to her at all, though he'd perversely tried to be.

Dancers were his first indulgence when he became successful, and Grayson sat through many a boring ballet until he found that he actually liked them. Then he would go backstage and treat an entire troupe to dinner while he tried to decide which one(s) he wanted.

He'd never seen a black ballet dancer before; he had to be honest. Yet the closest he could get to an obscene thought about her was setting her up with Dale.

He didn't know what the attraction experiment was for, and the results were equally as inconclusive.

He treated them to lunch, but it'd been so awkward that he left the two girls to catch up. Within earshot of course.

They were indeed very close. They were coiled up in a chair together, and they each helped with the task of re-twisting each individual strand of Amara's smooth dainty locs, which still took several hours even with the help of twenty nimble fingers. He knew because he periodically found excuses to bother them, during which all chatter unapologetically stopped.

On the plane, he noticed Amara didn't look like a mistress anymore or even a girlfriend. She looked like a billionaire's long-suffering wife.

No doubt she was suffering because of his jealous, drunken stupor from the night before.

He wished he could get the kind of drunk where he could forget the things he said, but he never could. To say it was spitting in the wind was not a powerful enough metaphor to describe how much insulting her had backfired on him.

It had been equal parts jealousy, stupidity, powerlessness, and self-sabotage. A dreadful combination he never wanted to feel again. He should've never agreed to go to Dale's with her. It was excruciating to him, a nauseating reminder that he should've left her alone from the beginning.

He had to find a way to make it up to her, but short of proposing to her, which he was positive she didn't want, he couldn't think of anything he hadn't already done. He was already having ominous premonitions that his efforts to end their affair on a positive note would crash and burn.

"I had no idea Montenegro was in the Balkans," Amara suddenly volunteered, dissipating his thoughts.

"It is," he lamely offered.

He didn't want to talk about last night.

She was right of course, about Dale.

But honestly, for the second— no third— time in Grayson's life, Dale had almost driven him to murder. Did he really try to accuse Grayson of not protecting Amara?

Fuuuuck you, Grayson thought.

The contract was Amara's idea, not his. He couldn't have laid the danger out any more clear than he had, the moment he agreed to sleep with her, and practically every moment after. He uprooted any attachments like weeds, but two would grow in its place. He'd tried to be a dick to her when it counted, but it only seemed to work when he *wasn't* trying. He was *obsessed* with protecting her.

Someone should, Dale had said.

God. He almost got his head ripped off.

The prank at the Malibu party had been personal. And the ninety minutes Dale had known Amara ahead of Grayson childishly ate away at him continually. At the party in Malibu, it had looked like 20 years to him, and even after the countless hours they'd spent together over three weeks, it infuriated him to see that same mysterious ninety minutes still existed between them.

The first time he'd had an inkling that he had hurt Amara, it was their first night together. The best day of his life, by a longshot.

Then she'd brought up Dale.

Dale who'd always had the best of both worlds. Dale who was valedictorian and homecoming king. Dale who could talk to computers and women. Dale who didn't bother about being good at sex because he was already good at love. Dale who could talk to Amara when Grayson could only cut off the impulse in order to survive.

Dale. The subject had caused him to shut her down, with restraint. At first.

And then last night he said... what he said. And he wanted to hurl himself right out of his panoramic window.

He didn't even know how he was doing it; he was just doing all the wrong things, all the time. It just snowballed.

But she'd served it right back to him, and he almost told her right then and there that he loved her.

Did he?

Maybe. Probably. He was drunk at the time.

But it felt true.

So there it was, he thought.

Not as cataclysmic as he believed it would be. It actually seemed quite rational to him. Too bad he had given Amara her fill of rational.

He'd discovered last week that she was looking into investing. She didn't hide it, but she apparently didn't want to discuss it with him.

Who was giving her the advice then?

More than likely Dale, her pal, and confidante, her bridge over the troubled water that was Grayson Davis. Grayson's mind drifted to the way she and Dale had looked at each other at the party like they shared a mutual burden in him.

Enough of this, he thought. He wanted to feel better and only Amara's come face would do.

"When we land we're going to Van Cleef's," he said.

"Jewelry?"

"Diamonds."

"You know those things are worthless, Grayson. Don't you watch movies?"

"It's my money," he protested.

"So you've mentioned," she sighed.

"You're not even curious?" he looked at her.

Her body went through a now familiar series of reactions to his gaze.

He wanted her. On this plane.

Should she let him off the hook?

What hook? This wasn't a relationship, she repeated in her head as if successfully brainwashed.

The real question was, was she in the mood to become a platinum card-carrying member of the mile high club right now or not.

"Okay, I'll bite," she smiled unconsciously.

Contract aside, she didn't want him to think everything was okay when it wasn't. But she couldn't retract her smile now.

She was rewarded with a wolfish grin.

Shit. He thought he was okay.

At least she knew he would be on his best behavior all day.

She shuddered.

Yep, that was definitely her mom she just heard.

Ridiculous. He'd never lay a hand on me, she thought.

There she was again!

"I'm going to buy a giant bag of loose diamonds," he began.

"Uh-huh," she urged, sounding disinterested.

"Then I'm going to take off all your clothes."

"I'm listening."

"Then I'm going to turn off all the lights and drape your brown skin in them."

Her mom probably never heard that one though, she thought. She can't be doing all bad.

"And then what?"

"And then...nothing. That's it. And then I'm gonna look at you."

She licked her bottom lip, stifling a smile. Her sunglasses gave nothing away of her eyes, giving them an air of aloofness. The combination was a complete turn-on.

"Wasteful," she simply said.

"No waste. Merely an exchange," he corrected her. *Wanna talk to me about investments now?* He thought.

"Still..."

"You love it," he teased.

Her smile was enough to adequately lift his spirits, so he let her alone. For the moment.

* * *

True to his word, he indeed bought a giant bag of loose diamonds when they landed. They had a free day before the summit tomorrow, and he was clearly determined to show her a good time. He pranked her no less than five times on the way to the hotel from the jewelry store, pretending to either have lost the bag or nearly spilled the contents down a random drain or out a window. Now it was his turn to laugh at her humorless face.

He wanted to wait until evening to cover her in the diamonds, but he gave up on the illusions of his slowly dwindling restraint. He found drawing the thick drapes in the hotel's penthouse suite were perfectly adequate.

They had a late lunch at the hotel's restaurant and then did some "lazy sightseeing," as Amara called it, where you don't plan anything you just walk around the city until you don't want to anymore. The city was like an untouched fairy tale in its golden earthy old world colors, and it stretched up and around them like a pop-up book. It was surrounded by water the color of his eyes, which was surrounded further by mountains. The sunny day was perfect, though it would've been enchanting in any weather. They took a boat ride. She reclined in his arms, and he sang her a song that she'd never before heard. She wondered what other things he was capable of doing that she had no idea of, songs that he knew that he would never divulge to her. She wanted to use the jaws of life to crack him open and climb in. A solitary tear flowed down her cheek, and he wiped it away.

That night she wore a dress that made them late to dinner.

It was floor-length, white, and had a daringly open back. When he saw her he told her she looked beautiful. Then he saw her from behind, and he said a curse. She laughed. They were just about to leave as he went to help her with her coat, and when he hesitated, he knew that she knew what he was thinking. He also noticed her eyes looked heavy in the hallway mirror. Her breathing became labored, and he could see her pulse quickening in her neck.

They hadn't had sex since... he tried to remember.

They'd fought the night before, and then he'd left her hanging on the plane. Then he draped her in diamonds, and that truly was it. He'd just looked at her. Then the boat ride...

Holy crap. He had inadvertently seduced her to within an inch of her life. His luck had changed.

Should he make her wait until after dinner¿

A quick gesture to the straps and the dress slumped dramatically to the floor.

Not a chance. He'd definitely screw it up between now and then.

When they eventually made it to dinner, every single eye was on her, and he swelled with pride.

She'd certainly made quite the journey from 2nd tier assistant to the project manager, now nearly a month ago. He would take credit, but he wasn't sure he'd done anything.

She was the single black face perhaps in the whole city, which garnered much them attention. If they knew who he was, they didn't draw attention to it.

And now she was unbelievably radiant and poised in her $3000 gown, ordering wine and handing off her coat graciously as if she were born to it. A dainty hand was holding up her chin, and her bottomless eyes glittered with a faraway look. Her hair was in a french twist. Her skin was smooth and flawless. She could've been 25, 100, or 1,000 years old. She caught his eye and his heart rate accelerated.

"What," she smiled, confidently.

He shrugged. What could he say?

"You're a vision," he answered.

She raised an eyebrow. "I'm a mess," she muttered.

He laughed. He knew what she meant. Not everything about her had changed.

After dinner, they walked hand in hand on the boardwalk. Hand holding meant a lot to her, he could tell. After a while, she was crying again.

"Don't do that, I hate it," he said.

"Why are you being wonderful right now?" she said.

"Why do I need a reason?" he asked.

"Is this your way of sending me off?" she questioned.

"Maybe," he conceded. "I don't want you to have a bad memory of me."

"Is that really for my benefit? Or yours?" she theorized rhetorically.

The luck had run its course, it seemed.

For the first time in his life, Grayson thought it best to keep his mouth shut.

* * *

At 5 am he was already awake, staring at Amara in the bluish-black light of the early morning.

The phone rang, and he whispered so he wouldn't wake her, "I'm awake already, thank you."

He definitely should've canceled his appearance at the G21 Leadership Summit.

Four weeks ago, there would've been no way he would've missed it. Now, the idea of spending three of his last five days with Amara, holed up in hours of symposiums and panels and glad-handing and trying not to doze off in front of C-SPAN was just... stupid.

Like they were really going to eradicate 3rd world epidemics, nuclear weapons, and world hunger *this* weekend.

Just because he was a successful billionaire didn't mean he had the answers. He started to feel a familiar old fatigue.

Once this summit was over, he was going to crash.

No part of him wanted to see Amara leave, but he was glad to have the incentive to send her away.

He didn't want her to see him like that.

It'd been a long time since the last one, right before Webster went public. And then Christmas had happened.

He hadn't been serious about killing himself. He was just... tired.

Of course, he didn't know that until immediately afterward. Until the vicious strangulation of his belt was so harsh, more unforgiving than anything he'd ever experienced. It felt as though that inanimate object was not only alive but evil and triumphant that its day had finally come.

Death would've likely been even more barbaric. And if Dale hadn't shown up, hadn't somehow known, Grayson would've found out first hand.

No. He didn't want to die. He was just... tired.

It was a valuable piece of information, strenuously attained.

He'd taken it easy after that, or so he thought. But maybe the stress had slowly gotten past his radar and crept back up again.

Pressures of success made life harder in some ways, but easier in the ways that used to plague him.

He thought maybe that part of his life was truly behind him, but it seemed he just couldn't outrun it. And now it had been simmering longer than it had ever simmered.

Had Amara sent it over the edge?

Probably. She was the most powerful kryptonite he'd ever encountered.

But he would have his last five days.

He needed Amara more than he needed to be okay right now, more than he needed to be strong. More than he needed to save the world.

* * *

The first day of the summit was a lot.

He spent the morning at a daily briefing, then all afternoon in a session on education in Myanmar, finally a grand symposium held in a formidable auditorium in the round, with stadium seats on all sides of the attendees. Grayson lounged at a distinguished, horseshoe-shaped conference table equipped with a microphone, and a laptop recessed in the surface for each seated member. Bono was there, so that was a big shocker. The founder of Magellan and his former boss, Daryl Jacobs was also there, a relationship once strained that he now enjoyed since he was a colleague and not his employer.

Jacobs incessantly took credit for birthing both Webster and MeTv at his company. Magellan had become a hydra in the years that passed, a slow development of which Grayson didn't much approve. But they supported Webster and made it seem as ubiquitous as Magellan itself. It would be years before he'd need to worry about competition.

The way he felt now, he could care less about the next five minutes of Webster. Not the best attitude to have at the G21 Leadership Summit. It was a good thing they didn't ask him to be a keynote speaker this year, or he would've absolutely had a breakdown.

"If sex trafficking isn't somewhere on this itinerary, then this whole thing is a giant, rich people circle jerk," Amara said when they were at dinner.

There was a flock of cameramen outside their window. The word eventually got out that "Gramara" was at the Summit. Thankfully the press was a lot more respectful in Montenegro.

Grayson sighed. "Don't, Amy. It's hard enough as it is to sit through this thing."

"So, don't."

"With great power comes great responsibility," he retorted between sips.

Amara in a strapless green number made a lewd gesture with her metaphoric penis.

"The cameras are right there, genius," he said.

"Since when do you even care about that?"

"I don't," he answered.

"So... stay home," she urged, somewhat selfishly. "You look spent."

"I don't have the luxury of just quitting my job when I get bored."

Amara casually looked up from her bite of food.

Grayson was finished, nursing a drink and engrossed with work on his phone.

"Like me," she prompted.

"Like you," he confirmed.

It wasn't even one of the bad ones. He didn't even bother to feel remorseful, she noticed.

But Amara was reaching her limit.

"So are you wiring me this money or what, because I don't think I'm ready to go back to the States just yet."

"Where are you going?" asked Grayson.

"I did a study abroad in Italy a few years ago. I kinda wanna see my old street. Eat crazy amazing food. Catch a movie even. There's a beautifully preserved old theater there."

No invite.

Did she even care that he was fluent in Italian?

"Want some company?" he ventured smoothly.

"Other than you? Yes." she curtly answered, taking a sip of their expensive Sauvignon Blanc.

Oh.

He knew he'd more than deserved it, but it hurt. Like hell.

They finished up in silence. Grayson left some crumpled notes on the table, and they braved the paparazzi as they were driven the short distance back to their hotel.

The next morning, there was a press conference. Grayson tried to focus, but all he could think about was Amara the millionaire, alone in Florence being ogled by about a thousand good-looking Italian men.

What did she mean by company other than him?

Shit. His insides were hollow. The flash of the cameras was enough to trigger a seizure. He just needed to get out of there.

He graciously bowed out of the world leaders' luncheon and raced back to the room, but Amara was nowhere to be found.

Of course, he thought. She hadn't expected him back for hours. Obviously, she wouldn't have sat around waiting for him to come back that evening so he could sneak attack her with insults.

He lay on the edge of the bed, relishing the quiet, letting the ceiling fan alleviate his humming mind.

60 hours left on the contract.

If he could make Amara smile today, all day, he would surely make it through the summit. And afterward, maybe he wouldn't return to the States either. He could find a jungle or a desert somewhere and just... scream. For a week. Maybe fight a bear or something. And then come back on a white horse and rescue Amara from her quality of life that would instantly plummet once he was gone.

He snickered and closed his eyes.

Just apologize to her you doofus, he heard a voice in his head that sounded conspicuously like hers.

It was worth considering. Maybe if he just apologized to her, his world could go back to normal. Amara was forgiving. But only to a point, and he had pushed that point. Maybe if he swallowed his pride, it would keep all this bile from coming up so frequently.

But to apologize would be a profound change in his convictions, and he was unwilling to do that. Amara could never be a permanent part of his life, so what would be the point?

Yes, he could see that he might love her, but she needed a better man— a belief that only grew over time since their conversation on the beach.

But he couldn't conceive of never seeing her again. Not yet. Yes, she'd become a habit by now, but she achieved that within the first week.

He simply would release her from this God-forsaken contract, maybe even put in a little extra for pain and suffering. Recharge, come back, and start again.

He relaxed. He had high hopes for his plan.

He just needed to be on his best behavior for the next 60 hours.

15

Chapter 15

For the second morning in a row, Amara woke up in bed alone. And for the second morning in a row, she cried.

Technically, it was the third, if 3 am counted as "morning."

The first was the night before the trip, the night of Dale's party, where he'd been so unbelievably hurtful. The second morning she cried because he'd been so heartbreakingly dreamy and wonderful, and she woke up to a cold bed, realizing that the fleeting glimpse of bliss was over.

The third morning was the worst, because for the first time it was because of something she had done.

He'd been a dick it was true. But something snapped in her. Right at the exact moment he was giving her what she'd wanted since that night on the beach. Since her first day at Webster. Hell, since her first school book report about him.

Want some company? he'd said.

A contract-free day with Grayson.

He told her, right to her face, that he wanted to be with her.

For him, it was a Say Anything moment.

And she'd sliced him open.

She could see she had hurt him, and what's worse, for about a second, it felt good.

And then... it didn't.

He trailed blood all the way back to their room. And when he rolled over to sleep instead of to hold her and make love to her, she retreated to the palatial bathroom, turned on every jet there was, cranked her iPod speakers, and cried her eyes out.

Somehow she'd slept, and when she finally woke up, it was almost noon.

She heard her phone buzz, and her heart jumped.

She knew it probably wasn't Grayson, saying, "You were right, I'm coming to rescue you and sing more songs to you in a boat." But she liked the thought. She waited a few minutes before she checked.

It was his assistant, Bryan.

You? Me? Mimosas? He wrote.

She smiled.

She wondered why she hadn't met Bryan until this trip and now she knew. He was tall dark, handsome, straight, and had one job in life which was to make Grayson's life as smooth as possible.

Grayson liked him because he wasn't even tempted to take on a relationship that would impede his job performance. But lately, Grayson was a little worried for him. He'd been his assistant for six years and refused to even let Grayson set him up.

Amara liked him because they could talk about their favorite subject, which was Grayson Davis.

She couldn't really talk to her girls about him anymore, because without context their opinions were always extreme and, whatever the opposite of cathartic is. She couldn't talk to Dale, because that was a can of worms she knew not to open anymore. Plus, she was starting to grow paranoid that they talked to each other about whatever she might've said to either of them.

So Bryan was a Godsend. He listened. He understood. Sometimes he actually had some good advice.

She sent him a message back.

Downstairs cafe in 30 mins.

* * *

"You got the day off today?" she began. She opted for a latte rather than a mimosa.

"No such thing as that, but no word from him today or yesterday," Bryan answered.

"Is that unusual?"

"Since you? No."

Amara smirked a little, though the words were starting to lose their impact.

"I'm all he needs to get by." Amara joked flatly.

"You're so low maintenance. I'm usually running around the city all day buying... stuff."

"Weirdest thing you ever bought for a girlfriend. Go."

"No contest," he shook his head after he'd taken a drink, "that one goes to Kimberly Diamante, Autumn 2014, she wanted a burger and fries, blended into a smoothie."

Amara shook with laughter. "You just made that up."

"I didn't," he simply said.

Amara couldn't stop. "You even talk like him."

"No, he talks like *me*," he clarified as he sipped his bright yellow mimosa.

"Ah. So who was he talking like before you, then?" Amara asked.

"You wanna guess?" he raised an eyebrow.

Amara took a stab in the dark.

"...Dale?"

"Dude! Dude! Dude!"

Amara was dying again.

Bryan liked Amara. He'd only known her through Grayson's requests for her, at first. When he found out that she was black he was pretty surprised, and even more surprised by the way he'd seen them together. It was as though the sun and moon had become human beings. Amara wasn't as hungry for PDA as some of his other mistresses, but anyone could tell they were unapologetically right for each other. And when he saw Grayson freely laughing and smiling he thought he'd entered a parallel universe.

Yet she'd seemed sad on the plane, sad in the car on nights after dinner. She'd lasted longer than any of his previous affairs, and Grayson seemed pretty attached to her. Yet she'd divulged to him that she was leaving in two days, right after the summit, and that Grayson already knew. He feared for what his job would turn into after she left.

"So you've got access to his accounts, right?" she confirmed.

"I do," he said, giving her a sideways look.

"Dude," she smiled. "I need you to do me a solid."

"I'm not going to get fired, am I?"

"Definitely not," she said, "but I need you to take me shopping."

* * *

By the time Amara returned from shopping she had a few hours to change before dinner.

She was a little worried that she'd shopped so long, and found so many things she was unwilling to put back. Goodwill prices these most certainly were not.

She told herself she would just buy enough good quality pieces to mix and match, but when the cashier rattled off the total she thought about how horrified her friends and family members would be if they knew what the damage was. Bryan had handed off the card to the cashier with a raised eyebrow. "I see you're starting to get your sea legs," he'd said.

Amara entered the elevator, scanned her key card, and pushed the penthouse button.

She had a feeling Grayson would say something similar if he saw her right now. But he wouldn't be back yet. Not for at least another hour.

Her afternoon with Bryan was a welcome distraction. She decided that when they got to dinner tonight, she was going to apologize and make it right. More importantly, she was going to take him up on his offer to join her.

So what, he was a hot mess. Honestly, what choice did she have?

If he really did want her, she was going to be wanted, by him, and that's all there was to it.

The room was completely dark when the doors opened. The shades had been drawn.

What the hell, housekeeping?

She saw a figure on the bed and frantically felt around the room walls for a light.

"Grayson??" Amara said, startled.

He wasn't asleep. He sat up.

He hadn't bothered to shave this morning. She'd never seen him with stubble.

Who was she kidding? She was never leaving this man. He was smiling devilishly.

"You're wearing jeans," he said.

She'd found the perfect pair and she couldn't bear to take them off once she tried them on. She dropped her bags and smiled at him fondly.

"You like?" she flirted.

"I do," he laughed.

She did a 12 point model turn for him. She was wearing a graphic shirt that was cut-off at the midriff. T-shirt and jeans, just like she'd wanted.

"They're doing a 90's retro thing here right now," she added.

"Come here," he said.

Like Pavlov's dogs, all systems were a go.

She sauntered over to him at the edge of the bed and he put his prickly face on her belly button. It tickled. She put her hands in his thick, now slightly too long hair. Suddenly he spun her around. She felt him grabbing her jeans at the waistband and then moving his hands across the taut fabric covering her backside. It was the stuff of dreams, he thought.

"I'm a fucking idiot," he said, and Amara laughed.

"Shall I take them off?" she offered.

"Do whatever you want," he said.

"Whatever I want?" she turned back around to face him.

He was looking up at her. He nodded.

He was so adorable when he nodded. She thought back to the first time she'd seen it, and it seemed like it was a hundred years ago.

"I want... to wait," she said.

He plummeted back to the bed as if he'd been shot in slow motion.

"Until when," he deadpanned.

"Not telling," she teased.

Grayson groaned as if he was a toddler being told it was bedtime.

"Dinner's in an hour, you big baby, what could we possibly get done before then," Amara announced on the way to the bathroom.

"Plenty," she heard a muffled yell through the bathroom door.

* * *

Dinner was...tense. In the best way.

Bryan had made a reservation at Solon, a Michelin-starred bistro that had come highly recommended. The venue used to be an old ballroom and theater. It housed large tables that had a gorgeous view of the city on one side, and a view of the magic brewing in the kitchen on the other. They were seated in a large sectioned-off area facing the water. Some of the attendees of the summit had also been dining there and they invited Grayson and his companion to join.

Amara pretended not to notice while Grayson kept his eyes glued to her. Other than a solitary arm reclined on the seat behind her, he was astutely keeping his hands off her, so as to follow orders as closely as possible.

"Your name has several meanings, do you know?" A conference member from Mumbai offered to Amara at the table.

"I was always told that it meant 'beloved,'" Amara said.

"It can," the man continued. "But it can also mean bitter."

"Latin," Grayson confirmed.

"An African girl in school told me it meant 'grace' in her language."

"No mystery behind my name," Grayson chimed in.

"What does it mean?" asked Amara.

"Son of the steward."

"Gray's son," said the man from Mumbai.

"The name could've meant 'turds,' and my mom still would've picked it because it sounded pretty," Grayson scoffed.

"I'm not sure I've ever heard you talk about your mom," Amara began.

"And you won't," he answered shortly.

Amara's smiling countenance waned. The other conference attendee graciously excused himself from the conversation as the two were awkwardly quiet. Even after he left, they continued sitting in silence.

"Is that supposed to entice me to delve further into you or something?" Amara suddenly blurted.

"No."

"Because it started off as mysterious, and now I just think the more people actually take the time to love you, the more you hate them."

Grayson sighed. "Do you want to have sex or do you want to start a fight?"

"Why can't I do both?" Amara protested.

"Because you can never recover after a fight," he retorted.

"I can never recover?"

"No. I say one off-color, yet true, thing and you're crying in your bathtub all night."

Amara's body tingled with rage.

"Ah," she simply answered.

"Yeah. There, I did it again, I guess? Which means no sex."

"If you say so. It's your dime, remember?" Amara replied stoically.

Grayson was losing patience with this incessant mantra of hers. The anger bubbled up and dissipated once it got to the calm sea of his face.

"I've never forgotten," he replied.

"Did you tell Dale about the contract?" she suddenly confronted him.

Grayson's body went rigid.

So her mind was drifting to Dale no matter where they went in the world.

Grayson calmly excused himself from the table and walked out of the VIP area, out of Amara's field of vision. The eyes in the room politely pretended not to notice Amara being left alone at the table by the CEO of Webster.

Amara became dizzy with frustration. Should she go back to the hotel? Should she just get on a plane and go home?

She had a profound sense that the money wasn't going to happen, like having fallen in a deep pit along a road and realizing you never told anyone where you were going.

A part of her felt weirdly ashamed that she seemed to be unable to suffer an emotional beating or two in exchange for a million dollars. Maybe the lifestyle had spoiled her, or maybe the man. But she sensed that she was not going to go any further.

She was actually going to break this deal just shy of 48 hours.

She was going to say something to him tonight, and he surely was going to say something, and whatever it was, would sever whatever connection they had left.

Instead of going to look for him, she decided she would just go back to the hotel.

She got up from the table wordlessly, trying not to indicate that she was leaving for good, even though she'd taken all her belongings. She wasn't in the mood for making up pleasant excuses to foreign strangers.

The bustle of the restaurant died down behind her as she headed down the grand spiral staircase that indicated the old ballroom's age, down to the ground floor lobby where she could contemplate whether to bother Bryan about the car or walk the moderate distance to the hotel. The plush carpet muted the sounds of her feet headed toward the exit.

But before she could make her way out the doors, she felt an arm grab her and pull her back behind the darkness of a long hallway, lit only by the glowing neon of the exit sign, and the moon showing through the sliver of glass in the exit door.

There was an old-fashioned curtain in front of the threshold, and he drew it, shrouding them in darkness.

She knew who it was, and she knew what he was doing.

What they were doing. About to do.

She was wearing a one-shoulder cornflower blue crepe dress with a slit down one side, and to him, she looked like some sort of delicious pie. And she was mad at him. So he had work to do.

But sex was what he was good at. It was the work part that he liked.

Before she could object he was on his knees in front of her, hiking her dress up to her waist and sticking his head in her crotch. He found that she'd already been wet a long time. He let out a curse as he smirked. She grabbed his head by the hair, gently yet firmly.

"You think you're hot shit now, don't you?" she said.

He smiled without looking up at her, and a gust of cold air hit her thighs. She shed her high heels, and he was eye level to her sex.

"Just make me come, asshole," she exhaled.

She watched by the silver of the moonlight as he basically made out with her body. He was kissing and licking and sucking, his head tilted and eyes closed, and his brow furrowed as if realizing he was in love, her left leg hiked up on his right shoulder.

Amara was moaning and cursing like mad. Her hips began rocking, his fingertips dug into her flesh. She was close to coming and she abruptly grabbed him by the hair again and made him admit that hers was the best, until she came down enough for him to continue.

She did this twice. At the third attempt, his hand left her hip and she heard the unmistakable sound of him unbuckling his pants.

Did he really plan on getting off that easy? Literally? The sound somehow gave her the fortitude to put off her own orgasm, though she was now at dangerous levels of arousal.

"Get up," she said. Slowly he stood, wide-eyed at this pissed off/turned on Amara hybrid. Before she could give him another order he had a firm hold of her face in his hands as he gently kissed her. He kissed her until he'd coaxed her tongue to come out from its hiding place. Her hands went to his chest, looking for his skin under his blazer, under his shirt.

Then she pushed, and his lips broke suction from hers.

He looked in her eyes. He was wholly unsure what she was thinking and wondered if he was on thin ice. The frenzied sound of their breathing reverberated through the hallway. He was rock hard and throbbing. He wanted to peel her dress down to her waist but he didn't dare move. He looked at her until her breathing had quieted and slowed.

Then she lowered her hands to his unfastened trousers, and his pulse was quickly on the rise again.

His left arm extended in front of him against the wall as Amara sunk to her knees. She undid the zip on his trousers and fished around his boxer briefs until she found a way to free his member effectively, indiscreetly.

If they were caught there'd be no mistake what they were up to. Grayson's other hand went to her jawline, elegant and pronounced in the scarce light of the glowing neon.

She was so, deliciously good at giving head. He seriously doubted that she was a novice at it.

Whatever. If he ever found the man he'd shake his hand.

She was being wickedly slow and deliberate about it, as though willing herself to be caught, and he let the tension she was brewing overtake him, though part of him knew he shouldn't. The more she dared him, the less willing he would be to stop if someone walked in on them.

Finally, he had to suck in a slow breath and toss his dizzy head back. His head came back down but it took another second or two for his eyes to roll back in place. He whispered vulgar encouragements to her and she responded with what she had available of her stuffed mouth.

With all his faults, Amara couldn't help the searing sensation in her heart whenever they were intimate. This was the man of her dreams. And in her dreams, she did whatever he liked, whenever and wherever he liked it.

For making her dreams a reality she felt she owed him a tremendous debt. That she was privy to him, to his faults at all, was sublime education however harsh, and he almost always chased one of those lessons with mind-numbing pleasure such as this, divulging how much he wanted her, how much he liked what she did to him.

She slurped and gulped until she was writhing in front of him. He had a bunched handful of her locs gathered up in his hand, one hand still steady on the wall. He forcefully tugged on her hair to wrench himself from her mouth and it was as though she was hypnotized by him, flicking her tongue at his taut erection. The hand in her hair went to his member and began to stroke. Now it was her turn to beg.

"You want this inside you?" he panted.

"Yes," she whimpered.

He repeated himself, his hand quickened its pace.

Amara became frantic.

"Say 'I want you inside me,' he said.

"I want you inside me," she repeated.

"Again," he said.

"I want you inside me!" she cried, pitifully.

"Get up. Turn around," he said.

Gingerly she did, and when her back was straight, she turned around and pressed both hands to the wall. She only heard the tearing of condom packaging.

When she moved her hands to the hem of her dress he rebuked her. A moment later he was sheathed and he slowly inched her skirt back up to her waist.

She was wearing a matching cornflower blue g-string. He would never be able to eat pie again without getting an erection, he thought.

In one smooth motion he was in. As he started faintly thrusting with her against the wall, Amara instinctively began to bend forward. He grabbed her hips, groaning at the sight of her bending to accommodate as much of him as she could. She was bending so far forward they nearly took up the entire hallway. She was so turned on that his thrusts were sending shocks through her entire body, all the way into her fingertips.

Slow and prolonged at first, he plunged himself into her cavernous depths again and again. She folded herself more and more until eventually she was bent over enough to touch her toes.

"Holy shit, Amy," his voice quivered, his pace still rhythmic. He gasped and winced and panted interchangeably, in disbelief at her daring position, at the depths of his own pleasure.

"You like that," she moaned, knowing the answer, knowing he was power-less to answer.

Irretrievably lost in ecstasy, he began slamming into her sharply. He was getting so deep she was exploding at every thrust.

"Yeah, give it to me," she could barely achieve a whisper through gritted teeth, she wanted to scream. She was sobbing, out of her mind with the velvety bliss he was sending all over her, all at once. She knew instinctively her orgasm would be intense and unforgiving. She should've been concerned about her own safety but she wasn't. At all. If they came at the same time she'd probably break her neck. Grayson was in the grips of primal madness, gasping and moaning with every thrust as if being dragged away by lust against his will.

Amara's orgasm seized her entire body and she let out a pinched squeal of uncontrollable "yes!" over and over, caring less and less about who could be listening the more he thrust into her convulsing sex. Focused on the intense pleasure still surging through her from his now frantic motions, her knees completely seized and he loyally held her together, his firm hands on each end of her hips clamped severely into her flesh.

For him, the end came soundlessly, jaw carelessly slack, his brow furrowed and dripping sweat down the bridge of his nose. Only the sounds of his final thrusts permeated the hallway. Their intermittent groans were staggered at first as his pumping slowed to a halt, and then their breathing and moaning gradually came in sync. He was swaying slightly and for a second he stumbled and put an arm out to steady himself.

"Fuck, I'm still coming," he announced.

Amara ground out a curse at that little piece of news, little fireworks going off in her belly as her body still held him captive.

Finally, they were free of passion's grip on them. Amara crawled her hands back up the wall until she was upright again. Grayson withdrew and collapsed onto the opposing side of the hallway, completely spent and beyond satisfied. She turned around and stood there in bare feet, still too wobbly to replace her shoes, smirking at his drunken appearance.

"Come kiss me," he finally said between pants.

"You can't be ready for round two," she breathed.

"I didn't get to kiss you at all."

She smiled. "Yes, you did."

"I don't remember," he exhaled, blankly staring towards the exit.

Amara giggled at him.

"Now, you may speak," he sighed, taking a breath.

Now she could speak? About what? She wasn't expecting "I love you," but "now you may speak" was an odd choice of words.

"What are you talking about?"

"Earlier. You asked me if I told Dale about the contract."

Amara stared at him, giving her head a quick shake in disbelief. He was hopeless.

"Okay... did you?"

"Yes."

Amara felt vomitous. Wasn't there a confidentiality clause in the contract? The contract from hell?

"When," she said. It was barely a question.

"Malibu. After I dropped you off, I went back to the party."

The Malibu party? The same night?

The contract didn't even exist yet. He'd given her a night to decide.

But then... he knew what her decision would be, didn't he?

And they'd laughed at her the whole month.

Well, Dale did, at least. Grayson didn't laugh much. Perhaps it stopped being funny to Dale the night of the party.

Or had it? Was that whole "I think he's in love with you" speech just a running gag between them?

Oh. *Now* she could speak. Because he knew what would happen when he told her the truth. And he had to have sex with her before the inevitable.

She wasn't even allowed to be outraged. She was prostituting herself after all, and he was a pragmatist.

She was, however, allowed to be mortified.

Amara was done talking. She put on her heels and click-clicked slowly out of the hallway. Grayson retreated to the bathroom and made himself presentable.

He felt like an apparition. He hadn't a single thought or an ounce of tension in his body, not even a helpful one.

He'd just easily had the best sex of his life. Amara, queen of the firsts. He even felt... had she cured him?

He smirked at the thought. He felt cured. The last day of the summit would be a breeze.

And why was he even stressed about the contract ending again? He could no longer remember. Now he would be free to woo her. He didn't quite know how to go about doing that, but his research skills were lethal. He suddenly couldn't wait to let her go.

While Grayson righted himself in the bathroom, Amara did the same and texted Bryan for the car. She didn't feel up to the walk.

She looked at herself in the mirror and her face crumpled at the reflection. She wept, quickly turning on the water in case he heard. Should she have it out with him?

Why? This. Wasn't. A. Relationship.

She had no upper hand, no bargaining chip.

All that would happen is that she would get hurt, or maybe she would land one, and he would get hurt, but that would still hurt her.

No. She wanted to leave. And she wanted to leave with nothing.

Because it was truly what she had.

16

Chapter 16

Later that evening, Grayson returned to his hotel room. Alone.
Every muscle in his body was now tense.

He paced. He panted. He fidgeted. Endlessly.

He was tired, but there would be no sleeping.

Amara had refused to come back upstairs.

The car ride had been a quiet one. When she got in the car, she looked as though she'd been crying.

Shit, he thought. He didn't want to admit that he'd divulged their arrangement to Dale, but he wasn't going to lie. He had every intention of making it up to her when they got back. He would draw her a bath. Maybe make love to her again, sweetly this time. Maybe even skip the first session of the summit and go with her to see the old church she'd told him about.

But then they entered the hotel lobby and he got into the elevator, startled when he turned around. She wasn't with him.

Scanning the lobby from the elevator car he searched for her, catching a glimpse of her and Bryan talking just as the doors were closing.

He'd pushed between the elevator doors just in time to exit. Amara had her back to him, but as he got closer he could see Bryan looked increasingly concerned. Their eyes met.

"Amara says she wants to go home. Right now." Bryan asserted.

Amara wouldn't turn to face him.

"Tell Amara, that it's pointless to fly the jet from here to LA twice in one day, and that if she wishes, we can leave tomorrow afternoon as soon as the summit is over."

She didn't speak, but he could see she was wiping away tears.

"She wants to book a flight back to the States tonight," Bryan said. "She found it online."

"Amara, that's ridiculous. The contract will be over while we're still in the air..."

"I'm going *home*, Grayson."

Oh.

Not his house "home." Not wherever he was "home."

A deep feeling of dread knifed his insides.

"Amy..." he started, "I'm sorry."

It was the first time she'd ever heard those words.

But it was too late.

She turned to look at him, her face swollen with tears.

"No, I'm the one who's sorry," she said. "I thought for sure I'd be good at this too, but... I'm not."

"But you are," he protested, "you're the fucking best at this," he tried to dissuade her.

"It's sucking my soul faster than any job ever did," she confessed.

"You want double?"

"Grayson—"

"Just... stay until the summit is over. I just need time to... stay until tomorrow, and you can double your money."

"I can barely stand the thought of keeping the money as it is," she said.

"No. This is not happening," he gritted his teeth, "you cannot, fucking do this."

Amara started backing away.

"I don't know what sort of deal you made, boss, but surely two days—"

"Shut the fuck up, Bryan. And if I find out that you so much as held her purse on your little shopping trip today—"

"I told you he would do this," Amara despaired.

He looked at the two of them. Bryan's eyes were sympathetic.

They hadn't slept together. But she'd now successfully formed alliances in his every direction.

"You fucking gold-digging bitch..." Grayson whispered, as if in amazement.

Amara slowly closed her eyes and let tears run as he berated her, quietly, smoothly, with immense skill. He told her how she would never get a penny, how he would die first, how his legal team would devour that lawyer friend of hers...

Grayson's mind forced itself back to the present.

Amara's shopping bags from earlier that day were on a table in the corner of the room.

His open hand suddenly found the neck of a table lamp. He reared it back high above his head and hurled it to the marble floor of the penthouse foyer where it shattered.

The noise replayed in his head like music. The lamp had been reborn into a constellation.

It bought him about five seconds of relief.

He went behind the penthouse's kitchen island, where he found the wine rack and mini bar and emptied them, carrying their contents to a desk in the bedroom where his laptop rested.

He opened it and started a spreadsheet.

If he started now, while the information was fresh, he could provide his lawyers a thorough accounting of the money he'd spent. The amount they'd agreed to, and why he was no longer obligated to pay it.

There was no way he would be able to sue her for damages. The contract was good.

But he could try. Litigation was a special hell.

The fidgeting got worse in front of the flickering laptop after an hour or two. He drank until he had to quickly retrieve the trash can underneath the desk.

He wasn't going to finish this tonight. Maybe ever. Hastily, he sent what he had to Amara's lawyer friend.

He suddenly couldn't sit down a moment longer. If he could just get reality to move past this excruciating moment...

He closed his eyes and raked his fingers over his face.

Things were about to get destroyed, and he could feel it.

He couldn't stop it. Which was good because he didn't want to.

He sauntered over to the table and flipped it over matter-of-factly, the shopping bags tumbled around him. He situated it flat side down, grabbed one of the table legs, and started to pull.

It was a damn good table. He needed more leverage. He obliged enthusiastically. The table leg snapped. The sound was soothing.

In the other meltdowns he'd had in his life, he never worried about what he damaged. But the first ones were in his shitty childhood home with the wood paneling, and anything he could've done to it was an improvement. The other was in the shitty apartment he shared with Dale and Bel. He felt bad that some of their stuff got inadvertently smashed, but it was nothing like this.

This was a beautiful hotel. And he didn't know how long he would need to go this time.

There would be no attending the summit tomorrow.

The meltdown was happening, and it was happening now.

* * *

The flight home on a commercial airline was grueling. As was Amara's grief.

He'd been right. The pain was excruciating. He was right about everything.

She was too embarrassed to call and ask Mya to pick her up the next day. Too ashamed to admit that she was coming home virtually empty-handed. She didn't even have the packed bag that she'd originally left with. Thank God Mya had retrieved the dress Amara had borrowed during her visit to Grayson's.

She'd had a 21-hour layover in Rome. Bryan had given her a hefty stipend and told her that he would suffer the consequences, should any arise. It was much more than a normal person would need. For a moment she thought about "roughing it" in Italy for a month with some of it, but after a night in Rome alone without Grayson, the idea quickly lost its appeal.

The next morning, Grayson was on the news in the airport, the anchor teasing a horrible tagline in the effort to keep the viewers glued to the set:

173

"Billionaire Meltdown."

Well, it'd worked. She nearly missed check-in waiting for the segment, which could only cite early reports saying that he hadn't attended the final day of the G21 summit and that he had been arrested.

Arrested?!

The flight home was unbearable. She barely slept, she was too timid to ask anyone for help, for a glance at their laptop, if they themselves knew anything more or even cared. She noticed a few extra long looks in her direction and became paranoid that they recognized her.

The moment the seatbelt sign had shut off on the plane, Amara reached for her phone.

When she turned it on, it warbled and burped as if possessed.

Grayson Davis was a trending topic everywhere. She read and read until she had to be kicked off the plane by a very polite flight attendant.

There were a ton of rushed, speculative articles about what had apparently happened in Montenegro after she left.

Some said it was drug-fueled, others alcohol, but they all used the same word to describe it: meltdown.

Only one from an otherwise disreputable online rag had theorized that a "Gramara" breakup might've been the catalyst, even citing a source that had seen a tense discussion in the lobby of their hotel.

But apparently, Grayson's "people," whom she knew was Bryan, had released a statement ensuring that their relationship had been stronger than ever and that she was supporting him through this difficult time.

Difficult time?

One report said that he'd been hospitalized.

Hospitalized??

She didn't know what to believe. She couldn't call, they never had each other's numbers. They only ever messaged each other online.

Should she even try? She didn't know if she still had access to his account. She didn't. The password had been changed.

Now she was afraid to even reach out to Bryan. He would've been the one to change his password. She understood, but she didn't want to find out she'd been completely cut out. Not like that.

The phone rang in her hand while she was investigating and she jumped. It was Kim.

"Girl... what in the hell..." was all she said.

"What?" Amara prompted.

"What did you do?" she accused.

"What do you mean?" Amara stammered.

Kim sighed. "Your boyfriend sent me... an invoice."

"Invoice?"

"He says you breached the contract, so you get nothing."

Amara choked back tears.

She was wrong; it was definitely too early to be dealing.

"I just realized that I don't want to talk about this."

"I'm gonna litigate his ass into the next millennium," Kim said.

"No you're not, no way will I help you do that," Amara insisted. She'd been to court before, and there's no way she would survive sitting in a courtroom with him doing everything he told her he would that last horrible night in Montenegro.

"I don't need your help," Kim countered.

"You need my permission. I'm the client, Kim."

"He can't just use you like that—"

"He didn't. I used him."

"You each used each other."

"Yes, and it was awful!"

"Then you *earned* that million, Amara," Kim argued.

Amara broke down then.

"I don't want it. Please don't make me fight for it," she sobbed.

Kim was silent for a long time.

"You the only person I know can turn trickin' into some complicated mess."

Amara managed a laugh.

"You hear he's in the hospital?"

"Yeah, but I don't know if that's true," Amara sniffed.

"It seems to be. He trashed the shit out of his hotel room, apparently. He didn't want to go, but they were going to press charges against him."

"What the hell..."

"Yeah, looks like you dodged a bullet," Kim said. "Rich people are crazy."

"Straight up," Amara scoffed dismissively, keeping her concerns to herself.

"I'm gonna send you this invoice though girl," Kim added.

"I don't wanna see," Amara said.

"Uh, no," Kim insisted, "you definitely need to see this thing."

* * *

Grayson didn't want to go to the hospital, but he didn't know much about Balkan jails. So the hospital it was.

Once he arrived there, however, he couldn't believe he'd ever resisted going.

First of all, they wheeled him around everywhere.

There was no sound, no light if he didn't want, and the meticulously timed intervals of constant, reliable beeps and warbles of machines were insistent enough to completely hijack his fraying mind. They fed him at the same regular intervals every day, and it was the same thing every day. He didn't talk to anyone, and if they tried, a very scary nurse would reprimand them in Serbian. He didn't make a single decision. About himself or anyone else.

And best of all, he wasn't home. In that house. The house that Amara built.

He was thankful that they hadn't elected to strap him by the arms. He didn't know how long they planned to keep him, and he didn't ask. Because he didn't care, couldn't care, about anything right now.

He couldn't even care that Amara was gone. *Good for her,* he thought. She hadn't taken a penny.

There's no way she'd have gotten home with whatever was in her pocket, so obviously, Bryan had helped her, likely with Grayson's own bank account.

Bryan hadn't known anything about the contract. But after that outburst in the lobby, he could've probably guessed. He thought back to Amara's calm tear-streaked face reacting to the sound of his words. He'd humiliated the woman he loved, and the memory made him reach for his breakfast tray. He thought for sure he would be sick as the words came unapologetically back to him verbatim.

He hoped Bryan gave him a good punch to the financial gut. Dale was probably giving him marching orders for now.

Grayson envied him. Because he'd risked getting fired to help Amara. He'd risked a big part of his life to help her— something Grayson had never done.

Did she reward him with a smile? With a hug? Something else?

He sighed. Whatever. It was done. He didn't need to hold on anymore. Amara deserved someone like Bryan.

Grayson always turned into Yoda on the other side of these meltdowns. Except for the last time he'd convinced himself that death was sure and hopeful.

It wasn't. So he had to be careful.

He'd been in the hospital two weeks before he got a visit from Dale, who looked terrible.

"You look like shit, dude," Grayson opined.

"I feel like shit."

"Sorry, man," Grayson said.

"What?"

"For having to put you through this. I know the press is probably a nightmare right now. And the board..."

"Actually, your publicist told the press you're getting help and that you and Amara are still together. They've pretty much died down. Did you just apologize?" Dale asked perplexed.

"Yes."

Dale left it at that for the moment. "The doctors think you have a high-functioning form of autism."

Grayson rolled his eyes.

"The same doctors that thought I was bipolar. And dyslexic."

"More like a completely different set of doctors entirely."

"What life-sucking drugs do they recommend," Grayson chided.

"None, and I actually agree with them."

"Dale Abernathy, M.D."

"I should receive an honorary one for living with you, dipshit." Dale continued, "It makes sense, Grayson. The behavior, the social... challenges. Your weaknesses, your strengths, your meltdowns—"

"Because the spectrum is so vast. Everyone seems autistic after reading a laundry list of random symptoms."

"So you think fuckin' bipolar is a better fit?" Dale asked, skeptically.

"No, I think they're all quacks and I don't want them anywhere near me."

"Grayson—"

"I'm just overworked," Grayson excused.

"So am I, but I'm not trashing my hotel room after I dump my girlfriend," Dale argued.

"That's because all your girlfriends are dogs, bro."

"You can't just joke this shit away anymore, Grayson. You're wearing a hospital gown right now."

"I'm not going to hurt myself or anyone else," Grayson sighed, exasperated.

"Normal people don't have to use that caveat," Dale said.

"It's not emotional at all, you know that. You've seen it. It's just stress. It's been, what, almost ten years since the last one? It's getting better."

Dale was silent for a moment before he began with the real reason for his visit.

"The board had an emergency meeting. They want you to step down as CEO."

"Dale—"

"I'm gonna take over. The workload is obviously too much for you," Dale continued, not listening.

"You came here to tell me you're muscling me out my own company? You're fucking Steve Jobs'ing me?"

"Dude, I can't save the narrative," Dale raised his voice. "It's fucked. Something has to happen."

Grayson was silent as he continued.

"You have a disorder. One that no one knew anything about when we were kids, but now, you actually have a chance to find out about yourself."

Grayson let his head roll to one side against the pillow.

"Or, you can insist that you're normal, and be the creepy guy that every girl on Webster is frightened of, who freaked out because he couldn't handle that his girlfriend left him."

"She breached the contract," he said.

"I don't want to fuckin' hear," Dale shook his head calmly.

"Two days left! She wouldn't listen to reason. I even offered to double it."

"I said I didn't want to hear."

"...An expectation was set." Grayson justified.

Dale got up to leave. "You're fuckin' autistic dude. And that's the angle we're going with, you no longer have control of it.

"Fine," was all Grayson said.

"Get ready to donate to every fuckin' autism foundation there is, bro. Don't be offended if they don't invite you to any summits. Unless you're prepared to buy real estate, because you're not demolishing another penthouse."

"I'm sure they're used to it," he said.

The two men looked at each other. Dale, as usual, was the first to laugh.

Dale rubbed his brow in fatigue. "I got another flight to catch."

"Take the jet."

"What will you do?"

"I can fly commercial, Dale. I'm not a recluse."

"Since when did apologizing start happening?" Dale suddenly resurrected the subject.

"I don't know, since... Amara, I guess."

Dale was taken aback.

"Wow. 'You guess'?"

"I had a lot to be sorry about," Grayson breathed.

"You love her," Dale stated. It wasn't a question.

"Yeah," he blinked, as if admitting he was terminal.

"What are you gonna do?" Dale asked.

Grayson slowly shook his head as though the prospect wearied him.

"I really... messed up. I knew this was coming I was just, trying to get her out of there before the worst of it and—"

"And lemme guess: you threatened her with breach of contract and she left anyway."

Grayson sighed. Dale knew him too well.

Grayson closed his eyes. "I'm gonna pay her, I just..."

"Why don't you just ask her to marry you?" Dale sounded confused.

"She... doesn't want that," Grayson explained.

"She's the only one that can put up with you and actually wants to," Dale protested.

"Not anymore."

Dale was frightened. What was so bad that even *he* knew he'd messed up?

"Oh my God, what did you do..."

"I sent her an invoice."

Dale stared. "An invoice."

"Yes."

"An invoice... for what."

"For... services rendered. And why she owes me," Grayson answered dryly.

Dale sat back down for that one. Grayson continued.

"It was... extensive. Twelve pages."

Dale completely lost it at that. He laughed, until he had tears in his eyes, about his hopeless friend. He was going to be stuck with this crazy bastard forever.

"Okay, well. Good luck with that, dude."

"When you were on the plane with her..." Grayson began.

Dale was earnest. "Grayson... I would never—"

"I know that," Grayson interrupted.

"Do you?" Dale's tone was accusing.

"She seems to think the two of you are friends."

Dale smiled. "You're a greedy bastard, you know that?"

Grayson suddenly felt sheepish. "You fuckin' had your hands all over her in Malibu."

"For fuck's sake," Dale laughed to hear that description, to hear his friend being possessive about a woman. And also to think of his stupefied look again. So priceless.

"She looks at you differently. I thought it was attraction at first, but... I think maybe it's trust."

Dale scoffed. "She shouldn't. I warned her about you, but I didn't know you'd fuckin' pay to sleep with her."

Grayson felt emotion flood his chest, regret chief among them.

"It seemed like a good investment. At the time," Grayson flatly admitted.

"I would judge you, but I threw money at her too. More than once," Dale shook his head. "She knows that I know. About the deal," he continued. "At my house—"

"When you were on the plane did you tell her about..." his voice trailed off as if he couldn't go on.

Dale knew what he was getting at. He should've felt insulted that Grayson thought him capable of bringing up Christmas with a random chick, but he was clearly in need of reassurance. Dale was sympathetic.

"I didn't bring up the past. At all." Dale assured him. "Literally all she talked about— all we talked about— was you. Whatever she feels for you, it isn't out of pity. Okay?"

With that, Dale was up out of his chair again.

"I'm sorry, Dale," Grayson stopped him as he stood in the doorway.

Two apologies in five minutes was a bonafide record. Dale didn't turn around as he asked, "About what?"

"That you had to be the one to cut me down. At Christmas."

Dale didn't move. He took a long deep breath.

"It's all right," he exhaled.

"I don't want to die anymore. I haven't for a long time."

"I know."

And with that, Dale was gone.

He knew that he and Dale understood each other. But the apology had affected him, Grayson saw.

When he sighed in the doorway, it was as though every bitter moment built up over their lives had been shed. Plus, Grayson indeed felt absolved, and it felt like a sanctuary after a decade-long storm. He suddenly wished he could've seen if some of the fatigue in Dale's face had somehow instantly lifted. Just to drive the point home. But there was no need. The experience was enough.

Perhaps there was something to this apology stuff. Yet another valuable piece of information. Strenuously attained.

* * *

By the end of week three, Grayson was regularly meeting with doctors as he agreed to therapy. He'd spent the week reading multiple research articles from medical journals. He color-coded the list of symptoms, dividing them into categories of Used to Have, Rarely Had, or Still Have.

Once he confirmed with his mother that he indeed had speech delays as a baby, he found that he either had or once had every single symptom on the list.

Amara's birthday had passed during the fourth week.

For her birthday, he called Bryan and had him wire transfer Amara a million dollars worth of shares in Webster stock.

He'd never stopped thinking about her. In fact, in his weeks of solitude, he was starting to wonder if his entire life was a culmination of a singular moment of meeting her.

He said himself he would've never approached her. And he hadn't, she'd worked at his company. He probably never would've called her into the conference room if he hadn't known of her obsession with him. And he would never have assumed that she could be interested in him at all if he hadn't already known it from her Webster page. And he wouldn't have visited her Webster page if he hadn't spoken to her on the phone.

What were the odds that she would be the one to answer? Not that astronomical to his calculations, only about 1 in 88. But still.

What were the odds that she would be an employee at all? At the heart of it, they were just two people in the wide world that needed a reason to meet, and the world had provided one. It was the single most serendipitous moment of his life. Because now he was here, the most uninvited, uncontrolled trajectory of his existence. In a hospital bed, being in love and getting help.

Love! It had caved in on him and made a spectacular mess of his life. He handled it about as poorly as a man could have. He was a miserable son of a bitch, and she navigated him and his universe like a fuckin' world-weary sea captain.

It made him emotional whenever he thought about it. What did a girl like her need all that strength for? He relived his blunders compulsively in the quiet. Would it really have been that terrible to let her get a little close to him? She ended up closer than anyone had any right to be in three weeks.

He wasn't good enough for her. But it occurred to him that he could try to be if he was truly inclined, and he was. He'd accomplished a great deal in his life, to be honest. Quite frankly he needed the challenge, and this one was sure to last. And it just so happened to be right around the time that a major puzzle piece to his life's context had fallen into his lap.

He wanted to tell her everything he'd learned about himself. Face to face. Amara, who made him laugh. Who cried at sunrises and job interviews and good sex. And hand-holding. Amara who was a visual feast he felt himself starting to crave again.

He would have to risk her either giving him the outcome he'd already accepted or freeing him from this jail of his own making.

He had to try and get her back. But how?

How did neurotypicals win the love of their lives back?

17

Chapter 17

I t'd been two months since Amara had last seen Grayson Davis, and it was not the way she liked to remember him.

But every time she remembered that day they met in the conference room, those eyes, that laugh, that instrument of exquisite torture that was his body, she inevitably would remember that night in the lobby of the hotel in Montenegro. The sound of his voice quaking in anger and tearing her down. The defeated way he'd apologized to her, had begged her to stay, in his way.

It'd been a cry for help, she now knew. He was breaking down, and he'd needed something constant, something familiar. And instead, she'd upended his entire world.

Since Webster had released the personal statement about Grayson's health and eventual resignation, Amara had looked up everything she could find about Asperger's Syndrome, and she researched in disbelief.

There he was, in black and white.

He didn't fit an abuse pattern. He fit an autism pattern.

His mood swings, his inflexibility about plans, the blunt way he spoke. The meltdown at the hotel. Even the way he would twirl her hair incessantly in bed, or the nights he didn't want to make love, he just wanted to look at her at night or in the early mornings. She wondered if it was his way of regulating his sensory input.

She wasn't quite sure where the amazing sex fit in, she thought as she smirked dumbly at her computer screen. But she'd been glad of it.

"Amara, stop daydreaming about Grayson's schlong, we have a pitch meeting," her new MeTV co-worker Alec startled her.

"I'm gonna have to review that sexual harassment section of the employee handbook," Amara said.

"I hear the code of conduct was much more lax at Webster," he said, before crossing his forearms to block Amara's feeble attack.

"Does he know you flirt with me?" Alec said.

"He's not threatened by you," Amara deadpanned.

No one ever released a statement saying they'd broken up, or that said relationship had only ever been a sexual contract. Whenever she was asked about it, either at work or by the occasional media outlet, she just shrouded it in the same request for privacy that the company had.

It was far from a clean break, but now that she was working for one of his good friends, Bel Hafiz, she'd already prepared herself for the eventuality of running into him.

She just hoped someone would give her a heads up before she'd have to lay eyes on him again and, God forbid, whatever new young thing he was with. If it was a blonde, she wasn't too worried. But she sometimes got a wave of nausea at the idea that she may have converted him. That there'd be some leggy, skinnier, lighter-skinned black girl on his arm. With good hair. Barf.

Neither party pursued the terms of the contract or its breach. Amara was too tired and embarrassed, and likely he was too. When Kim went behind Amara's back to contact Grayson's lawyers, they were oblivious.

The invoice had been... thorough.

He'd fairly acknowledged that she had more than fulfilled the contract and actually added $300,000 for what he branded "pain and suffering."

But the breach of contract was a whopping $1.8 million, as if putting it in big bold red letters could somehow justify the amount. So according to him, when it was all said and done she would've *owed* $150,000.00.

When she received it, she was horrified at first. He'd listed every sexual thing they'd ever done and assigned them monetary values.

All except her virginity, which had been cataloged "*Misc: loss of virginity,*

Cost: $0.00."

"Ugh," was all she could say. What a bastard.

Many things she hadn't remembered.

"*Eggs Benedict breakfast nook.*"

What?

Then she remembered he went down on her during breakfast once, and he had made her eggs benedict for the first time.

"I can't concentrate with you doing that," she'd told him.

"So don't," he'd said.

Why was he putting things *he'd* done on the invoice? What a noob.

She missed him.

She found herself reading through the invoice often.

A lot of things weren't sexual, and she was surprised that he'd remembered them, let alone valued them enough to put them on a spreadsheet.

"*Hand Holding, Qty. 37, cost: $3700.*"

It was purely Grayson-esque. It was sweet.

"Is Amara the only one with good ideas around here?" she suddenly heard, her train of thought dissipating like a cloud.

Just now they were in her Project Manager's office, a colorful, pop culture shrine of organized chaos, coming up with ideas for original content.

Each team member was given a camera and told to create their own channel for MeTV. The channel creator with the most views would become the team leader, but only for the quarter until they had the opportunity to compete again. Amara had won that quarter with her channel, which was just called "Dad Reacts." It was merely edited and uploaded clips of her father reacting to lynchpin episodes of popular TV shows.

Her dad was quite a character, and not only did she win the team lead position but her channel became one of the top 500 most watched. And generated revenue. She already had a few talk show ideas that she was holding back for herself that would likely ensure her team leadership for the rest of the year.

Amara. Loved. Her. Job.

And her job loved her. She goofed off the entire day and got pats on the back for it.

"Amara has a rich boyfriend why is she even here," her friend Maggie spat out.

"Can someone get me a drink?" Amara randomly said.

Everyone laughed. She was hilarious at MeTV.

Suddenly they all heard Bel's voice through the office speakerphone system, sounding foreboding.

"Is Amara in a pitch meeting with you right now, Kelly?"

It gave her butterflies like she was being called to the principal's office.

"She is," Kelly confirmed, tentative.

"Tell her to report to the balcony."

The balcony?

The MeTv headquarters was a massive cylindrical highrise that contained numerous levels of offices on the outer limits with a courtyard in the middle. Every office had a panoramic view of the grounds from the inside, and a view of the courtyard from the balcony. It was possible to get from the top level to the bottom via a giant spiral slide. It was a silly place to work.

Her meeting was on the sixth floor, so she had only to open the door to know what there was to see on the balcony. She looked down from the railing, and there was Bel Hafiz and Grayson Davis, founders of MeTv and Webster, sitting in the courtyard with a guitar, and for some reason, Grayson was wearing a black cowboy hat. Which was working for him.

When Amara walked out, wearing a long, oversized gray sweater that covered her hands, she instantly put her hand over her mouth and tried to turn around and retreat, but her entire team had gotten up and formed a bottleneck in the doorway. She gave up and walked toward the balcony's edge, now hiding her entire face with her sweater.

Co-workers who started to hear the ruckus began opening their doors to see what the fuss was about, and before long, the entire company was emerging from their offices to look over the balcony and gawk at Grayson Davis, actively involved in an elaborate romantic gesture.

Once there were as many eyes on them as could possibly be on them, he finally began.

"Amara Jean Riley," he said. "This is for you."

Oh God, did he really have to use her middle name?

She could barely see through her sweater, still over her face, but she heard Bel strumming a familiar 90's love song throwback...and now she understood the cowboy hat.

Was he really about to sing?

He was.

He did.

He barely got the first line out before whooping and hollering was heard around the entire workplace.

She was glad of that because he was not, by any stretch a singer. But what he lacked in talent, he made up for in confidence. Or was that just lack of social awareness?

It didn't help that Bel was encouraging it with his mediocre playing, and it dawned on her at some point that they had rehearsed this. Either recently, or some dorky thing they used to do when they were sharing an apartment. Both thoughts were equally horrifying.

The song was about love, and grappling with how best to tell someone that you love them. Grayson was speaking, nay singing, of love.

Had he loved her? For how long? Was it love— not jealousy or poor mistress etiquette— what made their affair so brutal and ill-fitting, so quick as a thought yet so long as a lifetime?

Certainly, she had hoped. She was beyond touched that he was now ready to acknowledge it to the world, let alone himself. She had no idea that he'd had the capacity to surprise her as much as he did. She hadn't known him as well as she thought.

To everyone else, the tears must've looked like a normal reaction to a grand gesture of love. Little did they know it was his first gesture ever.

The camera phones came out in earnest. Amara's uncontrollable smile was ear to ear behind her sweater sleeve, and when Bel got to the chorus and started singing harmonies, everyone erupted. Amara grabbed her immediate supervisor's arm and hid behind her shoulder, quaking with laughter.

Were they really going to sing the whole song? The moment seemed to go on for a million years. She both wished that it would and it wouldn't. She was glad that other people were documenting it because she was incapable of doing anything but be in shock.

She could only guess what was coming next. At the final chorus, the crowd joined in so that technically everyone was now singing to Amara. When Bel strummed the final chord, everyone erupted in cheers and applause.

In her heart, she knew what he was there to do, but she just couldn't believe it. Maybe he was just... there to... she couldn't find a way to make it safe. He could only be there to—

"Amara Riley," Grayson bellowed, breaking through her thoughts.

"Grayson Davis," she projected in a shaky voice.

"I am a spectacular asshole, and I'm sorry. Please forgive me, even though I don't deserve it," he pleaded, and the feminine sounds of "aww" filled the air. After a beat, he continued.

"These few months have taught me two things: one, I miss you. Two, I love you."

More ardent feminine sounds.

"Do you love me?" he asked.

Amara knew the answer, but then thought of their gorgeous and intense affair. The highs and lows were enough to make one seasick. She'd never truly been in a relationship with him.

What would a committed Grayson Davis look like? She had to find out.

Still, she made him sweat a little more before she answered.

"Yes."

The crowd was loving it.

"Amy," he felt confident enough to call her.

"What," Amy replied.

"Do you see yourself having a future here?"

Her mind shot back to that bizarre Monday morning in the Webster conference room, looking at eyes that were as familiar feeling then as they were now. She remembered the life-altering question and then she understood.

He was asking her to marry him. But also, he wanted to start over.

"Honestly?" she yelled.

"Of course," he smiled, his eyes glittering with emotion.

Should she say it? Now? Here?

It wasn't the answer he was looking for.

But the camera phones were still rolling. She'd have the moment forever. And everyone would love it.

Would he?

Ah, screw him.

Amara cupped both her hands over her mouth, and slowly articulated so that there would be no misunderstanding.

"We're having a baby!!" she shouted.

The office went into deafening raptures.

Grayson's face was blank, other than a faint grin. Bel shook him violently by both shoulders until his cowboy hat fell off.

She was going to try contacting him in another month when it was typically deemed safe to share the news.

She had to entrust Mya with the task of purchasing a test, in case stray paparazzi were lurking around. She hadn't even noticed that her period was late because up to then she was a virgin so why bother? She only noticed that she seemed to be coming down with something, and when the rest of the symptoms never came, only the fatigue, she still was oblivious. She had to look it up on Magellan.

It was either her thyroid, her vegetarian diet (which would never exist), or a baby.

The thought of being pregnant with Grayson's child thrilled her in the extreme. She had a permanent connection to him and every time she thought of it, which was about a hundred times a day, it brought a tear to the corner of her eye.

Whatever work that was going to be done today, it would not be done with the help of Amara.

The office shouting had only died down a little before she made it all the way to the bottom floor where Grayson was standing. It began again when she ran towards him and threw her arms around him. He felt new and real and familiar as she wept into his shoulder.

As she engulfed his senses he realized he'd yet to propose to her officially.

Did she even notice? He wrapped her quaking frame in his arms.

Tonight, he thought. She deserved more than one moment.

"I'm sorry," he said in her ear.

"I get it. It's okay," she assured him.

"I love you," he said again.

"You said that," she laughed.

He freed one of his hands to find her belly, and the "aww's" began again.

"Are you sure?" he asked, talking about the baby.

Amara nodded.

"Alright, everybody back to work!" Bel loudly announced. "Congratulations, Amara," he said, and there were a smattering of congratulatory echoes and applause before the electricity died down and the office went back to its business as usual.

"Can I have the tour?" Grayson said.

Bel overheard him and knew his friend too well.

"Behave, Davis..." he said, retreating to his office.

Grayson shrugged as if he didn't know what he meant.

Amara and Grayson left the courtyard hand in hand, walking lazily down the first-floor hallway.

"I don't have a job right now, is that okay?" he smirked.

Amara laughed. "Yes, I will support us."

"Did you get my birthday present?"

"I did," she replied, smiling. "Shares!! I'm such an idiot!" she lamented.

"Don't be too hard on yourself, it was your first sex contract," he giggled. "Anyone around here know that you're a multi-millionaire?"

"Only Bel," she dished, "everyone else just thinks I'm a gold digger."

Grayson laughed. He was looking at her mouth as they walked. He half whispered, "I want to kiss you but...we're supposed to behave ourselves."

Amara suddenly turned to wrap her arms around his middle.

"Screw him, it's been two months," she muttered.

"Is that how you talked about me when I was your boss?" he asked, his nimble hands searching for the bare skin under her sweater.

Their mouths made contact and instantly, predictably, they were transported.

Amara's heart went into overdrive, but she was prepared.

"I've been casing the joint for hiding places since I got here," her breath becoming labored.

He smiled into her neck, his lips tasting her scent.

"You knew I'd be back," he kissed.

"No," she breathed, smiling. "But I still couldn't help myself."

His blue eyes were ridiculously bright and present. She couldn't believe how radiant he looked as he said, "Lead the way."

Damn. This was her *man*.

Amara bit her lip, took his hand and tried to look nonchalantly as she led him down the hallway past the first-floor break room.

"Indoor or outdoor?" Amara smirked over her shoulder.

Grayson could barely believe his senses. Not only was her beautiful face suddenly within reach again, but she actually wanted to be his and genuinely seemed happy. And all without the stress of a contract.

At least, not a temporary one.

He didn't know the future, but for the first time in his life, he at least had tools.

He was resolved that Amara Davis would never know the same heartache as Amara Riley.

Grayson's limbs were as heavy as lead, and he was already breathless in anticipation. He returned her heady smirk with his own as he replied.

"Surprise me."

18

Epilogue

G rayson Davis was completely enthralled with Amara's growing belly. When he thought about his prior lifelong cynicism, it made him chuckle.

It was hard to watch his fiancée's stomach, now clearly someone's house, its occupant moving around discriminately to sound and touch and light, while still spouting ideals about population control.

Like most things new and daunting, Amara took to it like she had done it one hundred times. She'd looked forward to a water birth, but when her blood pressure skyrocketed a month early, she had to have an emergency c-section. For Grayson it had been a very scary twenty minutes of delivery that he did not want to relive, so Amara decided against broaching the subject of more children after their son Sam was born.

Once Sam was born, he and Grayson were virtually inseparable. Their nanny got paid to essentially watch Grayson watch the baby. Sam nursed and slept in precise intervals, and that fascinated Grayson. He was rather large for a premature baby. He had his mother's dark eyes and his complexion was a strict 50/50 compromise between the two parents. They fruitlessly debated on whose personality he had in infancy, each giving credit to the other. Grayson was already obsessed with monitoring his cognitive development, and so far it had only been five months.

They bought a new house in the Bay Area so that Amara could be closer to work and to the pediatrician she loved. Grayson carried on at Webster in an unofficial capacity and was still a member of the advisory board. He showed up at headquarters a lot more now that he lived closer, traveled less and, well, didn't work there anymore, much to Dale's vexation. Grayson always had the baby with him, and while initially darling it slowed the work pace to a crawl, which did not help his increased workload. Dale became CEO and Grayson hired the next COO, a former computer engineer who'd worked with them at Magellan, thus keeping it in the family.

Amara never considered herself competitive, but every quarter at work she fought valiantly for her position as team leader, and every quarter for a year she'd won, so they eventually just made her a project manager.

Now Amara was writing and editing her own talk show, interviewing some of her heroes and idols. They were now her friends and colleagues she'd collected through various fundraising events for autism research, and parties she'd attended with Grayson and Dale. The series was shot at MeTV headquarters, and had become popular enough that she could probably focus on it full time if she wanted to.

But she couldn't imagine herself quitting just now. She loved her job and couldn't bear to leave it unless she could up and take the entire sixth floor with her.

Besides, with a five-month-old, editing was not something she could give more time to than she did, and she was too much of a creative control freak to let someone else do it.

Her most popular episode to date was the interview she'd done with her own husband, the only one he'd ever agreed to after the public "meltdown," and the most revealing one he'd likely ever do. True to Amara's style it was informative yet silly, engaging and also irreverent, respectful and revealing.

"Mr. Davis," Amara began the interview.

"Mrs. Davis," Grayson smirked.

"You were supposed to be my first interview," Amara said.

"I was," Grayson said.

"And you told me no."

"I did."

"And then I was mad at you."

"Not unusual."

"Because I'd already told everyone that I could get you, and it was in the bag."

"Your fault," Grayson answered bluntly.

Amara let out a huff of air. "An early lesson learned, yes. But then I got over it because... do you remember what you told me?" Amara asked, for the sake of the video. Grayson never forgot a conversation.

"I said that you don't need me to make the show successful."

"And you were right."

"And I was right. Also, not unusual," he added.

Amara shook her head, mouthing the word "no" to the camera.

The morning she shot the interview with Grayson, Amara still had an entire half day left of work. It should've been spent editing and working, but ended up of course being filled with quietly performed sex acts while the blinds were tightly drawn, and also discussing matters of the wedding, which had been postponed until after their son was born. Amara had insisted on the legal nightmare that was the prenuptial agreement— most likely, he suspected, to appease his family. Now the big day was weeks away.

Amara lay in Grayson's arms on the comfortable couch that used to be in Mya and Amara's house in Palo Alto, now the place where the collaborative magic happened in Amara's spacious office. The slow, steady cacophony of rain was pelting the panoramic window. Baby Sam could faintly be heard on the nanny cam that was live streamed from MeTv's in-house daycare.

Grayson's eyes were closed, his pants unbuckled, his breathing now steady and slow. The rhythm of the rain completing his post-coital bliss.

"How am I supposed to make it through an entire wedding without tearing the dress off of your body," he asked matter of factly.

"It's a real problem," Amara admitted.

Amara and Grayson had slowly become addicted to making love at inappropriate times and places, especially after the baby. So far they'd never been caught, and their perfect record had made them bold. And sloppy. Moreover, starting Monday they were planning to abstain until the honeymoon, which they had mutually agreed should technically begin *right after* the minister says "You may now kiss the bride."

"Both our slightly horrible sets of parents will be there, we could try to focus on that."

Grayson's father had made an unfortunate comment about baby Sam's complexion when they were visiting at the hospital.

Before that he'd made another comment towards Amara's dad at their penthouse when they'd had a small gathering to celebrate their engagement. He'd been a fan of her dad's through Amara's channel, so no one could quite tell if he'd meant to be complementary or not.

Meanwhile everytime Amara's dad came around he asked Grayson if he could "borrow" money, and Amara had to distract him from going into stories about his marriage to her mother, oblivious to the fact that he was an abusive lunatic. At least their mothers were both champions in the small talk Olympics.

"If my dad says something racist at our wedding then I'm definitely going to rip your dress off," Grayson said.

Amara snickered.

"And they're sewing me into it, so if you rip it, there's no going back."

"I think I'll be fine as long as the dress isn't white," he quipped. Amara gave him an elbow to the ribs.

"I think I'll be fine, as long as you're not dirty talking me during the slow dance like you did at the engagement party," Amara muttered.

Grayson smiled, touching his tongue to his teeth at the recollection.

"Maybe... after the reception? It's not as classy, but we could get the stretch limo instead of the Rolls..." she suggested.

"Mm. So roomy," Grayson smirked.

"Then you see where I'm going with this," Amara giggled.

"Admit to me right here and now that you were giving blowjobs before me," Grayson suddenly confronted Amara. "I won't be angry, I promise."

Amara giggled. "I can't because then I would be lying," Amara replied absent-mindedly.

"There's no way," Grayson insisted.

"Did you ever think that maybe I'm a natural?"

"No such thing."

Amara laughed. "Okay, so maybe I did have some tutelage."

Grayson looked down at her intrigued.

"My girl taught me," she said.

"The one who hates me," Grayson differentiated.

"She doesn't hate you anymore. That much. And no, not Mya."

"The lawyer who wanted to sue me."

"That's the one."

"How did your best friend, who I'm starting to love more and more, teach you to give blowjobs."

"It's stupid and involves bananas."

"I'm on the edge of my seat," he replied.

Amara smiled as she sighed.

"She just told me to practice on a peeled banana and try not to use my teeth."

"And how many bananas were harmed in this endeavor before you figured out what you were doing?"

Amara laughed. "Not many, actually. Kim said if I was slobbering uncontrollably then I was doing it right."

"I'm gonna nominate your friend for the Nobel Prize."

More laughter from Amara.

"I can do that, you know. As a billionaire."

"Really?" Amara asked curiously.

"No," he giggled.

Another elbow.

"So... when exactly did you begin this self-taught course of yours," he asked.

"Honestly?" Amara flirted in a low tone.

"Of course," Grayson gave it right back to her. He was ready again.

"Right around the time I spoke to one Travis in Quality Control."

Grayson beamed as his eyebrows went up.

"And just what were your intentions towards this Travis in Quality Control?"

"I was gonna find him and give him the business," Amara mumbled.

"Maybe one day you still can," Grayson stated innocently, his blue eyes dark and playful.

Amara looked down at his lips. She was ready again too.

"Well when he shows up, tell him I said to wear the cowboy hat," Amara whispered as she went in for another slow, transportive kiss.

Sneak Peek to Book 2: Mya's Pride

Mya

Amara serves us dinner in the kitchen around the massive island rather than the grand dining room table. Two giant pendant lamps on each side of it light the kitchen like candlelight. I can see the starless night in the skylight above that's about the size of the island itself and lined by gorgeous mahogany box beams. I can't believe my friend lives in a house with a kitchen like this. It's even more gorgeous during the day, when the skylight alone lights the entire kitchen. Amara just walks around like it's all normal.

She insisted on cooking and made salmon, my favorite dish of hers. Grayson's here, of course, being completely sexy with the baby on his lap. Rosetta, the nanny, is supposed to be taking a much-needed break but is instead cleaning, which isn't her job.

Dale, his best friend and the new CEO of Webster, arrived home with Grayson. I've only met him twice before: once when Amara had her engagement party and once when Sam was born.

Dale is the whitest white guy I've seen up close in a long time. The fact that he's filthy rich makes him almost bioluminescent. He has a bit of swag to him, that I suppose comes with being a billionaire and simply existing in the presence of Grayson Davis, who's also pretty white. He seems like an underdeveloped character in a story, who's talked about a little and shows up even less. He's wearing a light blue dress shirt with white cuffs, navy slacks, and an expensive gold watch. His dandruff commercial hair has grown out rather long since I last saw him, and it's kind of amazing. Full and sort of gravity-defying. He probably owned the 90's.

He's a big deal now that he's the CEO of Webster. It's weird to see him gussied up on the cover of magazines as I'm in line at the grocery store. *I watched a baby throw up on him*, I think to myself. He's a busy guy, always having to run. So it's even weirder to see him sitting down, not wearing his coat and enjoying a meal.

He's kind of scattered and immature, a contrast to Grayson's aloof and measured air, but I'm slowly finding out that he and Grayson are self-made for a reason. They're both about a little older than we are and it shows. I have no idea what they're talking about at dinner, but they more than know, and even though they're a bit too old to just be pretending like we're not there, I have to admit the exchange is fascinating. Dale is matching Grayson idea for idea without the slightest hiccup. They're in a mind-meld.

"Anyone ever tell you that you talk waaay too much, Mya?" Dale addresses me suddenly, throwing me a bone. He and Grayson talked business virtually the entire time while Amara and I sat quietly.

He's doing that thing again. That weird uncle routine. I expect any moment he'll pull a quarter out from behind my ear.

I slowly shake my head. The corners of my mouth droop.

"Nope," I reply, trying to be ironic, but it falls flat. Not even Amara has my back. She's busy with the baby.

"You know, Mya," Dale begins through sips of wine, "I took ballet when I was a kid."

"You don't say," I feign wonder. Grayson and Amara look at each other, roll their eyes and scoff.

On the now three occasions we've met, Dale has brought up this fact every time, as though he's never brought it up before. At first, I— an *actual* ballet dancer— was polite in pretending that he's never mentioned it, but at some point, it became obvious that it was a running gag.

"Yes, my mother was a ballet teacher, and all three of my sisters were ballerinas," he continues.

"Uh-huh."

"And eventually, I got tired of just sitting there watching them, and I started learning the stuff myself."

"Get the fuck outta here," I say wide-eyed, sounding stunned. That gets a laugh from Grayson. My heart flutters.

"Yes," he says as if trying to convince me, "and I was the only boy in the class," he goes on.

"It happens," I reply.

"Grayson was there, he can attest," he continues, getting Grayson in on the gag.

"Only because Leslie never wore a skirt," Grayson smirks as if reminiscing.

"Did your mom ever dance professionally?" I ask.

"She did, but she met my dad in her 20's, so she never went further."

"As in, she quit."

Dale thinks for a moment then slowly nods his head.

"And did your sisters ever get their pointe shoes?"

"No," Dale scoffs as if the notion was impossible some reason that only he knew about. "They didn't stick with it that long."

"So your sisters were never, in any capacity, ballerinas then," I say.

I look Dale squarely in the eyes as I speak. My air is cool, my eyes devoid of malice, demanding merely an admission of the truth. Dale is just about to surrender when Amara breaks in.

"Mya's hardcore about her profession," she fills in for context.

"Nope, not 'hardcore.' I'm just being 'regular core' right now," I insist.

"Do you ever think about what you'll do once it's over?" Grayson asks.

Amara gives him a sharp look.

"Grayson..." she reprimands.

"No, it's okay," I assure her, bringing up one leg in my chair so that I'm hugging it. "My two goals in life were to be either a principal or the lead in Swan Lake and the Nutcracker Suite, and after this fall I'll have done it. And I'll probably hang it up after that."

Amara frowns, "You never told me that."

I slowly nod.

"So that's it?" she laments.

"It has to be it," I say, taking a drink of wine, "I've done more than I ever thought I would. And I love performing, I love pushing my body to the limit, but now I'm 27 and I know I can't do this much longer." I leave traces of lipstick on my goblet, the color of the wine.

"So what will you do after that? Teach?" Grayson asks.

"Maybe. Open up a little ballet school for black girls or something."

"Just for black girls?" Dale inquires.

Oh, here we motherfuckin' go.

I give him the benefit of the doubt and explain myself. "Um... maybe other minorities too, but I know first hand how underrepresented black girls are."

"You wouldn't be open to teaching—"

"No," I cut him off. I silently pick at my plate until I settle on a bite and bring it to my mouth. The subject isn't closed. But if Dale wants to go, I'm ready.

I'm grateful to come from a proud black college-educated family, doing well enough to afford to support my passion for ballet from the time I was five years old.

In return for their investment, I worked hard, never missed a lesson, even if I was sick, and made a habit of learning others' parts in the event I had to step in. These habits and more opened the door for my unique opportunities as a black ballet dancer.

It was no easy feat because I've been told over and over by very blunt, very Russian teachers that I would never be able to make it a career. That I was too dark, too shapely, too short, too muscular, too whatever else to see my dream realized.

Meanwhile, my white counterparts only adequately trained, barely had finish in their technique if at all, and never suffered the challenge of having to prove wrong the very people that were supposed to be supporting them. No wonder they never got better.

Yes, there were plenty of places for little white girls to line up and learn to be mediocre for the rest of their lives and cry because they had to stand in line next to the one black girl in the class. I have no intention of adding to their numbers.

"Fair enough," Dale says after a slightly awkward silence.

"Don't say it if you don't believe it," I challenge.

"No, I believe it's fair. I'm just sad that my son or daughter may not have the benefit of having you for a teacher," he offers, subtly making his point.

"Get Kim pregnant this weekend and you just might," I can't help sneering.

Amara snickers and lowers her head to the table.

"I'm lost," Dale says.

"Kim says she wants to get pregnant by one of you," Amara clarifies.

"Oh," Dale simply says. "The one who was suing you, right?"

"That's the one," Grayson says.

"What does she look like again?"

Amara gets up from her chair to swat Dale.

"What?" he innocently protests, not bothering to shield himself from her harmless taps.

"She's tall, light-skinned, and completely gorgeous," I fill in for him.

"Really?" Dale sounds intrigued, and I kind of want to rip out his throat.

"Her mom's a crackhead prostitute though, so. Buyer beware," I add caustically. Amara looks at me.

"What, did I tell a lie?" I ask innocently.

"You've been like, majorly cranky today," Amara glares.

Majorly cranky. I guess that's one way to sum up my complete and utter discomfort with this entire situation since the day I got that call in the middle of the night. Talkin' 'bout "he wants me to be his mistress and so do I." While everyone smiles and laughs about it.

"You know, I think I'm just way out of my routine," I say instead. "I can't remember the last time I didn't practice for two days in a row."

"You're on hiatus for the summer, aren't you?" Grayson remembers.

"Yeah but I still go to lessons in between. My yoga class starts when I get back."

"You do yoga too?" Dale politely asks.

"I teach it, yeah. In the summer."

"My goodness," Dale marvels.

"She's a hustler," Amara adds about me. "And she does hair."

"You're like wonder woman." Dale compliments me.

I'm annoyed with this white man and I don't know why. I don't know what

I want from him— if anything— but his gratuitous compliments are not it.

"On that note, I think I'm gonna turn in early," I say.

"Already??"

"Yeah, since I'm cranky and all, I think I'm going to fit some exercise in before bed."

"Okey-doke!" Amara says, trying to ignore my shifting mood, which sounds much worse than it actually is.

But I hate that she's acting like she doesn't know that about me already. Is that for their benefit?

"Can I come wake you up?"

"Yeah, girl," I say on my way up the stairs, trying to sound buoyant.

"Okay goodnight," Amara projects up the stairs.

Dale

There's silence at the table until we're convinced Mya's out of earshot.

"Yikes," I say once she's gone.

Amara gives me a glaring look.

"What?"

"Why are you grilling her about black ballet studios?"

"I wasn't grilling her."

"Do you know how much shit she got her entire life, even from her own family, for wanting to dance like a 'white girl,' for going to Julliard instead of Alvin Ailey?"

"I wasn't grilling her!"

"Nina Simone went to Julliard," Grayson interjects.

"Babe, don't be sexy right now, I can't," she says, sounding genuinely irritated.

"Sorry," says Grayson.

"Honestly, I think no matter what we talked about tonight she would've bit my head off," I say.

"She did not 'bite your head off,' Dale, get a grip," Amara snipes. "Just because she's not on her knees in front of you after your stupid joke...."

"I could've been catching up at work, I really don't need this," I close my eyes and sigh.

"Why is everyone melting down three days before my wedding?" Amara whines, panicky.

"Because no one here is having sex." Grayson points out.

"Damn," I shake my head.

"Omigod, you're right," Amara realizes. "How come everyone's melting down now *except* you?" she asks Grayson.

"Excessive masturbation," Grayson deadpans. He makes sure I'm taking a drink when he says it. I nearly make it, but then I look up to see Grayson looking directly at me and I choke.

Amara is faintly amused when she says, "I'm going to go feed the baby, so if you two nerds will excuse me..."

"Good night Amara," I send her way as she heads up the stairs with Sam.

"Excessive masturbation?" I smirk.

"Excessive," Grayson repeats and I snicker against my will. Now that Amara's gone, Grayson and I talk even more freely.

"Speaking of which... is Mya still a virgin?" I ask.

"How should I know?"

I tilt my head and give him a look.

"In your expert opinion," I humor him.

"Oh. Yeah, pretty sure she is. What, you couldn't tell?"

"No. She kind of seems like she had a bad one and now hates all men."

"I think she's just afraid that at any moment, a random penis is just going to come out of nowhere and fuck her, and then she'll have waited this entire time for nothing," Grayson flatly states. My head drops with guilt as I try to keep my laughter quiet, shoulders quaking.

"It's a valid fear," I say when I finally recover. Grayson smiles.

"And now she's going on a trip to Spain with the likes of us," Grayson muses. His meaning is not lost on me.

I never considered myself a playboy, but add Grayson and Bel to the mix and my game becomes lethal, especially considering we're worth almost a 150 billion collectively. We're like a Voltron super robot of sex.

Or at least, we were. I'm sure Bel and I could do fine on our own.

"And Bryan," I quip. Grayson laughs. We often joke that Bryan is quite possibly the latest model android passing himself off as human.

"Obviously you'll have to take me out of the running," he says.

I grimace. Again, his meaning is not lost on me.

"Dude, there is no 'running,' because I'm not touching that with a ten-foot pole."

Grayson shrugs, grinning. "We'll see," he says.

"Uh, no we won't," I insist with a knitted brow, slightly offended at his suggestion. That somehow he knows me better than *I* know me. I only like cranky bitches when Bel and I are wasted, and also while I'm 20 years old. So seeing as how I'm 34, and there's probably going to be a gaggle of pre-approved paparazzi there, I'll probably be on my best behavior at this wedding.

Still, my pulse quickens as the blood pumps through my body anyway. The mental trigger has become all too routine. Anytime the three of us were together, without fail it meant that someone was about to get fucked. I didn't know if Grayson the family man would change the dynamic, but Grayson was apparently of the opinion that it wouldn't.

"Guarantee you she's already thinking about it," Grayson goads me. I pretend not to notice. "You're really gonna let Bel sleep with her?" he asks.

"She would punch Bel in the face," I say.

"Bel has the least amount of shame out of all of us."

"This conversation has turned very disturbing," I squirm. I'm fighting off a smattering of naughty images as it is, after Mya talking about pushing her fucking body to the limit. I don't want to envision the inevitable fallout of Bel emotionally scarring one of Amara's best friends.

"Hey, you brought it up. I'm just being practical."

Damn, he's right. I did bring it up.

"Well," I sigh after a sip of wine. "Let's just say I'm having enough trouble losing my own virginity to worry about someone else's."

"It's been that long, huh," Grayson says.

"It's grown all the way back, bro."

Grayson huffs a laugh. "Fuckin' dry spells. Literally the worst thing about being single, I can't believe I ever thought that life was better."

Suddenly I'm feeling exhausted, and Grayson's "hashtag blessed" musings are not helping.

I only ever had one romantic objective in my life, and that was to find a woman to adore.

I'm romantically obsessive-compulsive. Sure, I run through a lot of duds, but I have a hard time leaving stones unturned.

And when your best friends are playboy billionaires, well. There are a lot of stones.

I raise my wine glass to make a toast.

"To getting laid in Spain."

Grayson raises his beer bottle.

"I will most definitely drink to that," Grayson says as our chuckling mingles with the clink of meeting glass.

* * *

Go to C.L. Donley.com to get the entire Billionaire's Club Trilogy!

I Love Reviews!

Yes, even the critical ones (sort of)! Did you like the book? Which part was your favorite? Was it too steamy? Not enough? Anything stand out to you that you've never read before, or haven't seen in awhile? Anything you could've done without, perhaps? Well I wanna know!!

Besides, when it comes to choosing the next great read, reviews can make or break, whether you're an indie author like me, or one of the big fish in a New York Publisher's pond. I'm a stay at home mom with a limited budget, looking to support myself and my family with my dream.

Believe it or not, you can help. A LOT.

And all it will cost you is about a dozen words or more.

If you enjoyed this book at all, and think others should too, please take five minutes to leave this book a review on the page of your respective ebook retailer. Thank you!

Copyright

Acknowledgments

To H.S., without whom this story or its universe would not exist.

About the Author

C.L. Donley lives in Texas with her husband and three small children. She spends her days daydreaming, reading, perusing social media, watching YouTube and/or Netflix, and occasionally writes books in between.

You can connect with me on:
- 🌐 https://cldonley.com
- 🐦 https://twitter.com/C_L_Donley
- 📘 https://facebook.com/amarascalling
- 🔗 https://bookbub.com/authors/c-l-donley

Subscribe to my newsletter:
- ✉️ https://www.subscribepage.com/CLDMLLanding